Designs On Murder

A Ghostly Fashionista Mystery

Gayle Leeson

Grace Abraham Publishing

Gayle Leeson
Grace Abraham Publishing
A Division of Washington Cooper, Inc.
13335 Holbrook Street
Bristol, Virginia 24202

Publisher's Note: This is a work of fiction. Names, characters, places, and incidents are a product of the author's imagination. Locales and public names are sometimes used for atmospheric purposes. Any resemblance to actual people, living or dead, or to businesses, companies, events, institutions, or locales is completely coincidental.

Book Layout ©2017 BookDesignTemplates.com

Ordering Information:
Quantity sales. Special discounts are available on quantity purchases by corporations, associations, and others. For details, contact the "Special Sales Department" at the address above.

Designs On Murder/ Gayle Leeson. -- 1st ed.
ISBN 978-0-9967647-6-6 (Paperback)
ISBN 978-0-9967647-5-9 (eBook)

Also by Gayle Leeson

Down South Café Mystery Series

The Calamity Café
Silence of the Jams
Honey-Baked Homicide

Kinsey Falls Chick-Lit Series

Hightail It to Kinsey Falls
Putting Down Roots in Kinsey Falls
Sleighing It In Kinsey Falls

Victoria Square Series (With Lorraine Bartlett)

Yule Be Dead
Murder Ink

For Tim, Lianna, and Nicholas

A girl should be two things: classy and fabulous.

— COCO CHANEL

Contents

Chapter One

A flash of brilliant light burst from the lower righthand window of Shops on Main, drawing my attention to the FOR LEASE sign. I'd always loved the building and couldn't resist going inside to see the space available.

I opened the front door to the charming old mansion, which had started life as a private home in the late 1800s and had had many incarnations since then. I turned right to open another door to go into the vacant office.

"Why so glum, chum?" asked a tall, attractive woman with a dark brown bob and an impish grin. She stood near the window wearing a rather fancy mauve gown for the middle of the day. She was also wearing a headband with a peacock feather, making her look like a flapper from the 1920s. I wondered if she might be going to some sort of party after work. Either that, or this woman was quite the eccentric.

"I just came from a job interview," I said.

"Ah. Don't think it went well, huh?"

"Actually, I think it did. But I'm not sure I want to be doing that kind of work for...well...forever."

Gayle Leeson

"Nothing's forever, darling. But you've come to the right place. My name's Max, by the way. Maxine, actually, but I hate that stuffy old name. Maxine Englebright. Isn't that a mouthful? You can see why I prefer Max."

I chuckled. "It's nice to meet you, Max. I'm Amanda Tucker."

"So, Amanda Tucker," Max said, moving over to the middle of the room, "what's your dream job?"

"I know it'll sound stupid. I shouldn't have even wandered in here--"

"Stop that please. Negativity gets us nowhere."

Max sounded like a school teacher then, and I tried to assess her age. Although she somehow seemed older, she didn't look much more than my twenty-four years. I'd put her at about thirty...if that. Since she was looking at me expectantly, I tried to give a better answer to her question.

"I want to fill a niche...to make some sort of difference," I said. "I want to do something fun, exciting...something I'd look forward to doing every day."

"And you're considering starting your own business?"

"That was my initial thought upon seeing that this space is for lease. I love this building…always have."

"What sort of business are you thinking you'd like to put here?" Max asked.

"I enjoy fashion design, but my parents discouraged me because—they said—it was as hard to break into as

{ 2 }

professional sports. I told them there are a lot of people in professional sports, but they said, 'Only the best, Mandy.'"

Max gave an indignant little bark. "Oh, that's hooey! But I can identify. My folks never thought I'd amount to much. Come to think of it, I guess I didn't." She threw back her head and laughed.

"Oh, well, I wish I could see some of your designs."

"You can. I have a couple of my latest right here on my phone." I took my cell phone from my purse and pulled up the two designs I'd photographed the day before. The first dress had a small pink and green floral print on a navy background, shawl collar, three-quarter length sleeves, and A-line skirt. "I love vintage styles."

"This is gorgeous! I'd love to have a dress like this."

"Really?"

"Yeah. What else ya got?" Max asked.

My other design was an emerald 1930s-style bias cut evening gown with a plunging halter neckline and a back panel with pearl buttons that began at the middle of the back on each side and went to the waist.

Max caught her breath. "That's the berries, kid!"

"Thanks." I could feel the color rising in my cheeks. Max might throw out some odd phrases, but I could tell she liked the dress. "Mom and Dad are probably right, though. Despite the fact that I use modern fabrics—some with quirky, unusual patterns—how could I be sure I'd have the clientele to actually support a business?"

"Are you kidding me? People would love to have their very own fashion designer here in little ol' Abingdon."

"You really think so? Is it the kind of place you'd visit?" I asked.

"Visit?" Max laughed. "Darling, I'd practically live in it."

"All right. I'll think about it."

"Think quickly please. There was someone in here earlier today looking at the space. He wants to sell cigars and tobacco products. Pew. The smell would drive me screwy. I'd much rather have you here."

Hmm...the lady had her sales pitch down. I had to give her that. "How much is the rent?"

"Oh, I have no idea. You'll find Mrs. Meacham at the top of the stairs, last door on your left. It's marked OFFICE."

"Okay. I'll go up and talk with her."

"Good luck, buttercup!"

I was smiling and shaking my head as I mounted the stairs. Max was a character. I thought she'd be a fun person to have around.

Since the office wasn't a retail space like the other rooms in the building, I knocked and waited for a response before entering.

Mrs. Meacham was a plump, prim woman with short, curly white hair and sharp blue eyes. She looked at me over the top of her reading glasses. "How may I help you?"

"I'm interested in the space for rent downstairs," I said.

"You are? Oh, my! I thought you were here selling cookies or something. You look so young." Mrs. Meacham laughed at her own joke, so I faked a chortle to be polite. "What type of shop are you considering?"

"A fashion boutique."

"Fashion?"

"Yes, I design and create retro-style fashions."

"Hmm. I never picked up sewing myself. I've never been big on crafts." She stood and opened a file cabinet to the left of her desk, and I could see she was wearing a navy suit. "Canning and baking were more my strengths. I suppose you could say I prefer the kitchen to the hearth." She laughed again, and I chuckled along with her.

She turned and handed me an application. "Just read this over and call me back if you have any questions. If you're interested in the space, please let me know as soon as possible. There's a gentleman interested in opening a cigar store there." She tapped a pen on her desk blotter. "But even if he gets here before you do, we'll have another opening by the first of the month. The web designer across the hall is leaving. Would you like to take a look at his place before you decide?"

"No, I'd really prefer the shop on the ground floor," I said.

"All right. Well, I hope to hear from you soon."

I left then. I stopped back by the space for lease to say goodbye to Max, but she was gone.

I went home—my parents' home actually, but they moved to Florida for Dad's job more than two years ago, so it was basically mine...until they wanted it back. I made popcorn for lunch, read over Mrs. Meacham's contract, and started crunching the numbers.

I'd graduated in May with a bachelor's degree in business administration with a concentration in marketing and entrepreneurship but just couldn't find a position that sparked any sort of passion in me. This morning I'd had yet another interview where I'd been overqualified for the position but felt I had a good chance of getting an offer...a low offer...for work I couldn't see myself investing decades doing.

Jasmine, my cat, wandered into the room. She'd eaten some kibble from her bowl in the kitchen and was now interested in what I was having. She hopped onto the coffee table, peeped into the popcorn bowl, and turned away dismissively to clean her paws. She was a beautiful gray and white striped tabby. Her feet were white, and she looked as if she were wearing socks of varying lengths— crew socks on the back, anklets on the front.

"What do you think, Jazzy?" I asked. "Should I open a fashion boutique?"

She looked over her shoulder at me for a second before resuming her paw-licking. I didn't know if that was a yes or a no.

Even though I'd gone to school for four years to learn all about how to open, manage, and provide inventory for a small business, I researched for the remainder of the afternoon. I checked out the stats on independent designers in the United States and fashion boutiques in Virginia. There weren't many in the Southwest Virginia region, so I knew I'd have something unique to offer my clientele.

Finally, Jazzy let me know that she'd been napping long enough and that we needed to do something. Mainly, I needed to feed her again, and she wanted to eat. But I had other ideas.

"Jazzy, let's get your carrier. You and I are going to see Grandpa Dave."

Grandpa Dave was my favorite person on the planet, and Jazzy thought pretty highly of him herself. He lived only about ten minutes away from us. He was farther out in the country and had a bigger home than we did. Jazzy and I were happy in our little three-bedroom, one bath ranch. We secretly hoped Dad wouldn't lose the job that had taken him and Mom to Florida and that they'd love it too much to leave when he retired because we'd gotten used to having the extra space.

I put the carrier on the backseat of my green sedan. It was a cute car that I'd worked the summer between high school and college to get enough money to make the down payment on, but it felt kinda ironic to be driving a cat around in a car that reminded people of a hamster cage.

Sometimes, I wished my Mom and Dad's house was a bit farther from town. It was so peaceful out here in the country. Fences, pasture land, and cows bordered each side of the road. There were a few houses here and there, but most of the land was still farmland. The farmhouses were back off the road and closer to the barns.

When we pulled into Grandpa Dave's long driveway, Jazzy meowed.

"Yes," I told her. "We're here."

Grandpa Dave lived about fifty yards off the road, and his property was fenced, but he didn't keep any animals. He'd turned the barn that had been on the land when he and Grandma Jodie bought it into a workshop where he liked to "piddle."

I pulled around to the side of the house and was happy to see that, rather than piddling in the workshop, Grandpa was sitting on one of the white rocking chairs on the porch. I parked and got out, opened the door to both the car and the carrier for Jazzy, and she ran straight to hop onto his lap.

"Well, there's my girls!" Grandpa Dave laughed.

It seemed to me that Grandpa was almost always laughing. He'd lost a little of that laughter after Grandma Jodie had died. But that was five years ago, and, except for some moments of misty remembrance, he was back to his old self.

I gave him a hug and a kiss on the cheek before settling onto the swing.

"I was sorta expecting you today," he said. "How'd the interview go?"

"It went fine, I guess, but I'm not sure Integrated Manufacturing Technologies is for me. The boss was nice, and the offices are beautiful, but...I don't know."

"What ain't she telling me, Jazzy?"

The cat looked up at him adoringly before butting her head against his chin.

"I'm...um...I'm thinking about starting my own business." I didn't venture a glance at Grandpa Dave right away. I wasn't sure I wanted to know what he was thinking. I figured he was thinking I'd come to ask for money--which I had, money and advice—but I was emphatic it was going to be a loan.

Grandpa had already insisted on paying my college tuition and wouldn't hear of my paying him back. This time, I was giving him no choice in the matter. Either he'd lend me the money, and sign the loan agreement I'd drafted, or I wouldn't take it.

I finally raised my eyes to look at his face, and he was looking pensive.

"Tell me what brought this on," he said.

I told him about wandering into Shops on Main after my interview and meeting Maxine Englebright. "She loved the designs I showed her and seemed to think I could do well if I opened a boutique there. I went upstairs and got an application from the building manager, and then I went home and did some research. I'd never seriously considered opening my own business before--at least, not at this stage of my career--but I'd like to try."

Another glance at Grandpa Dave told me he was still listening but might take more convincing.

"I realize I'm young, and I'm aware that more than half of all small businesses fail in the first four years. But I've got a degree that says I'm qualified to manage a business. Why not manage my own?"

He remained quiet.

"I know that opening a fashion boutique might seem frivolous, but there aren't a lot of designers in this region. I believe I could fill a need...or at least a niche."

Grandpa sat Jazzy onto the porch and stood. Without a word, he went into the house.

Jazzy looked up at me. *Meow*? She went over to the door to see where Grandpa Dave went. *Meow*? She stood on her hind legs and peered through the door.

"Watch out, Jasmine," he said, waiting for her to hop down and back away before he opened the door. He was carrying his checkbook. "How much do you need?"

"Well, I have some savings, and—"

"That's not what I asked."

"Okay. Now, this will be a loan, Grandpa Dave, not a gift."

"If you don't tell me how much, I'm taking this checkbook back into the house, and we won't discuss it any further."

"Ten thousand dollars," I blurted.

As he was writing the check, he asked, "Have you and Jazzy had your dinner yet?"

We were such frequent guests that he kept her favorite cat food on hand.

"We haven't. Do you have the ingredients to make a pizza?"

He scoffed. "Like I'm ever without pizza-makings." He handed me the check. "By the way, how old is this Max you met today? She sounds like quite a gal."

"She doesn't look all that much older than me. But she seems more worldly...or something. I think you'd like her," I said. "But wait, aren't you still seeing Betsy?"

He shrugged. "Betsy is all right to take to Bingo...but this Max sounds like she could be someone special."

First thing the next morning, I went to the bank to set up a business account for Designs on You. That's what I decided to name my shop. Then I went to Shops on Main and gave Mrs. Meacham my application. After she made sure everything was in order, she took my check for the first month's rent and then took me around to meet the rest of the shop owners.

She introduced me to the upstairs tenants first. There was Janice, who owned Janice's Jewelry. She was of average height but she wore stilettos, had tawny hair with blonde highlights, wore a shirt that was way too tight, and was a big fan of dermal fillers, given her expressionless face.

"Janice, I'd like you to meet Amanda," said Mrs. Meacham. "She's going to be opening a fashion boutique downstairs."

"Fashion? You and I should talk, Amanda. You dress them, and I'll accessorize them." She giggled before turning to pick up a pendant with a large, light green stone. "With your coloring, you'd look lovely in one of these Amazonite necklace and earring sets."

"I'll have to check them out later," I said. "It was nice meeting you."

Janice grabbed a stack of her business cards and pressed them into my hand. "Here. For your clients. I'll be glad to return the favor."

"Great. Thanks."

Next, Mrs. Meacham took me to meet Mark, a web site designer. Everything about Mark screamed thin. The young man didn't appear to have an ounce of fat on his body. He had thinning black hair. He wore a thin crocheted tie. He held out a thin hand for me to shake. His handshake was surprisingly firm.

"Hello. It's a pleasure to meet you, Amanda." He handed me a card from the holder on his desk. "Should you need any web design help or marketing expertise, please call on me. I can work on a flat fee or monthly fee basis, depending on your needs."

"Thank you, but—"

"Are you aware that fifty percent of fledgling businesses fail within the first year?" he asked.

I started to correct his stats, but I didn't want to alienate someone I was going to be working near. I thanked him again and told him I appreciated his offer. It dawned on me as Mrs. Meacham and I were moving on to the next tenant that she'd said the web designer was leaving at the end of the month...which was only a week away. I wondered where he was taking his business.

The other upstairs shop was a bookstore called Antiquated Editions. The owner was a burly, bearded man who'd have looked more at home in a motorcycle shop than selling rare books, but, hey, you can't judge a book by its cover, right?

I made a mental note to tell Grandpa Dave my little joke. As you've probably guessed, I didn't have a lot of friends. Not that I wasn't a friendly person. I had a lot of acquaintances. It was just hard for me to get close to people. I wasn't the type to tell my deepest, darkest secrets to someone I hadn't known...well, all my life.

The brawny book man's name was Ford. I'd have been truly delighted had it been Harley, but had you been expecting me to say his name was Fitzgerald or Melville, please see the aforementioned joke about books and covers. He was friendly and invited me to come around and look at his collection anytime. I promised I'd do so after I got settled in.

Then it was downstairs to meet the rest of the shop owners. The first shop on the left when you came in the door--the shop directly across the hall from mine--was Delightful Home. The proprietress was Connie, who preferred a hug over a handshake.

"Aren't you lovely?" Connie asked.

I did not say I doubt it, which was the first thought that popped into my brain, but I did thank her for the compliment. Connie was herself the embodiment of lovely. She had long, honey blonde hair that she wore in a single braid. Large silver hoops adorned her ears, and she had skinny silver bracelets stacked up each arm. She wore an embroidered red tunic that fell to her thighs, black leggings, and Birkenstocks. But the thing that made her truly lovely wasn't so much her looks but the way she appeared to boldly embrace life. I mean, the instant we met, she embraced me. Her shop smelled of cinnamon and something else…sage, maybe.

"Melba, that blue is definitely your color," Connie said. "By the way, did that sinus blend help you?"

"It did!" Mrs. Meacham turned to me. "Connie has the most wonderful products, not the least of which are her essential oils."

I could see that Connie had an assortment of candles, soaps, lotions, oils, and tea blends. I was curious to see what all she did have, but that would have to wait.

"I'm here to help you in any way I possibly can," said Connie, with a warm smile. "Anything you need, just let me know. We're neighbors now."

Mrs. Meacham took me to meet the last of my "neighbors," Mr. and Mrs. Peterman.

"Call us Ella and Frank," Ella insisted. She was petite with salt-and-pepper hair styled in a pixie cut.

Frank was average height, had a slight paunch, a bulbous nose, and bushy brown hair. He didn't say much.

Ella and Frank had a paper shop. They designed their own greeting cards and stationery, and they sold specialty and novelty items that would appeal to their clientele. For instance, they had socks with book patterns, quotes from famous books, and likenesses of authors.

After I'd met everyone, Mrs. Meacham handed me the keys to my shop and went upstairs. Although my shop wouldn't open until the first of September, she'd graciously given me this last week of August to get everything set up.

I unlocked my door and went inside. I was surprised to see Max standing by the window. I started to ask her how she'd got in, but then I saw that there was another door that led to the kitchen. I imagined my space had once been the family dining room. Anyway, it was apparent that the door between my space and the kitchen hallway had been left unlocked. I'd have to be careful to check that in the future.

But, for now, I didn't mind at all that Max was there. Or that it appeared she was wearing the same outfit she'd been wearing yesterday. Must have been some party!

"So, you leased the shop?" Max asked.

"I did!"

"Congratulations! I wish we could have champagne to celebrate."

I laughed. "Me too, but I'm driving."

Max joined in my laughter. "I'm so glad you're going to be here. I think we'll be great friends."

"I hope so." And I truly did. I immediately envisioned Max as my best friend—the two of us going to lunch together, talking about guys and clothes, shopping together. I reined myself in before I got too carried away.

I surveyed the room. The inside wall to my right had a fireplace. I recalled that all the rooms upstairs had them too. But this one had built-in floor-to-ceiling bookshelves on either side of the fireplace.

"Does this fireplace still work?" I asked Max.

"I imagine it would, but it isn't used anymore. The owners put central heat and air in eons ago."

"Just checking. I mean, I wasn't going to light fire to anything. I merely wanted to be sure it was safe to put flammables on these shelves." I could feel my face getting hot. "I'm sorry. That was a stupid thing to say. I'm just so excited—"

"And I'm excited for you. You have nothing to apologize for. How were you supposed to know whether or not the former tenant ever lit the fireplace?"

"You're really nice."

"And you're too hard on yourself. Must you be brilliant and well-spoken all the time?"

"Well...I'm certainly not, but I'd like to be."

"Tell me what you have in store for this place," she said.

I indicated the window. "I'd like to have a table flanked by chairs on either side here." I bit my lip. "Where's the best place around here to buy some reasonably priced furniture that would go with the overall atmosphere of the building?"

"I have no idea. You should ask Connie."

"Connie?" I was actually checking to make sure I'd heard Max correctly, but it so happened that I'd left the door open and Connie was walking by as I spoke.

"Yes?"

"Max was telling me that you might know of a good furniture place nearby," I said.

"Max?" Connie looked about the room. "Who's Max?"

I whirled around, thinking Max had somehow slipped out of the room. But, nope, there she stood...shaking her head...and putting a finger to her lips.

"Um...she was....she was just here. She was here yesterday too. I assumed she was a Shops on Main regular."

"I don't know her, but I'd love to meet her sometime. As for the furniture, I'd try the antique stores downtown for starters. You might fall in love with just the right piece or two there." She grinned. "I'd better get back to minding the store. Good luck with the furniture shopping!"

Connie pulled the door closed behind her as she left, and I was glad. I turned to Max.

"Gee, that was awkward," she said. "I was sure you knew."

"Knew?"

"That I'm a ghost."

Chapter Two

I realized I was gaping and closed my mouth. My legs felt weak, and I looked around for somewhere to sit.

"Windowsill," Max said, pointing behind me. "Your scrawny butt will fit just fine."

I backed up until I felt the windowsill against my thighs, and then I sank into a sitting position.

Max came and sat beside me. "I honestly thought you knew. I mean, how could you not?"

"How could I not? You're as clear to me as Connie or anyone else in this place."

"Really?" She clapped her hands together. "How delightful! I mean, I knew yesterday when we met that you were special. I thought you realized you had a...well, a gift...or a sensitivity...or whatever you want to call it."

"No...I...no." I shook my head slightly. "This isn't an elaborate joke you guys are playing on me, is it?"

"Afraid not. Connie doesn't know I exist. I have tried to get her attention a few times. Despite all her talk about chakras and crystals and energy, she has no clue. Neither does anyone else here. Until you."

"Wow."

"I'm truly happy you're here. I haven't had a friend in almost a decade," she said. "You can't imagine how boring it is not having anyone to talk with. And it's so frustrating trying to read books, magazines, or newspapers over someone's shoulder when that person has no idea you're there. I seldom get to finish anything." She scoffed. "And don't even get me started on those books upstairs."

"How—if you don't mind my asking—did you...?"

"How'd I die? Fell right down those stairs out there and broke my stupid neck. It was May of 1930, and I was going to a dance. I was wearing this beautiful new gown—" She indicated the dress she was wearing. "—and nobody even got to see me in it! The last time anyone saw me in the flesh, I was wearing that godawful monstrosity Mother buried me in. It was truly the kind of dress you'd take one look at and say, 'I wouldn't want to be caught dead in that.'" She shrugged. "Thanks a million, Ma!"

"I'm truly sorry."

"Me too. I'd have much rather had a closed casket with a photo of me looking beautiful sitting on the lid or on a table beside the coffin. I did not appreciate people peering down at me." She shook her head. "The dress was this muddy-water brown with no frills whatsoever. I've had over eighty years to try to figure it out. At first, I thought that Mother bought the dress to save money. But that makes no sense. I had plenty of gorgeous gowns in my closet. She didn't have to buy anything new. And everything I had looked better than—"

"I meant I'm sorry that you're dead," I said.

"Oh." She waved away my concern with a flick of her wrist. "That's all right. I'm used to it. We can still be friends, can't we?"

"Of course."

"I'm glad. Some folks are prejudiced against people who are…well…different."

I smiled. "I know. I'm…I'm happy we're friends."

"So am I. We're going to have such fun together. Do you have anything we could read?"

"I've got lots of things we can read."

She gave a little round of applause. "Swell! I'd hug you if I could."

I giggled, and I wasn't quite sure if I was delighted, hysterical, or a little of both. "For now, I need to get to the antique store to see what I can find."

"Yeah. I'd love to go with you, but I'm kind of confined to this building."

"Kind of?" I asked.

"I can go out onto the porches, but that's about it. I'm looking forward to seeing what you find in the way of furniture." She grinned. "You're going to make this place fantastic. I just know it."

"Thanks." I stood on legs that were still a little unsteady. "I'll be back either later today or tomorrow."

I didn't go on downtown to the antique shops. Instead, I drove as slowly as I could to Grandpa Dave's house. He was the only person I could think of who could possibly listen to my story without thinking I was I completely insane. Still, I went at a snail's pace so I could think of what and how to tell him. I hadn't come up with a good story by the time I got to his house.

I knocked on the front door and then sat on the porch. It was a hot, sunny day, but the shaded porch provided some relief from the heat, and the swing gave me something to do.

Grandpa Dave came outside and sat on his usual white rocker. "Would you like some water or sweet tea?"

"Maybe in a few minutes."

"You've got that look on your face."

"What look?" I asked.

"The look you'd always get when you were a little girl and something had happened that you weren't quite sure about. You'd always talk with me about it before deciding whether or not to tell your mom and dad."

I smiled slightly. "And whatever it was often stayed between you and me."

"That's right."

Grandpa knew me well enough to sit quietly until I was ready to confide in him. Finally, I just blurted it out.

"Max is a ghost."

"All right."

"All right? You don't even sound surprised."

"Well, it is historic Abingdon," he said. "Everybody with an old building supposedly has a ghost or two."

"But, Grandpa, I saw her plain as day...and we talked the same way you and I are talking right now! And then, I mentioned her to Connie, but Connie couldn't see her."

"Now you're getting ahead of me. Who's Connie?"

I filled Grandpa in on how I'd gone this morning and spoken with Mrs. Meacham and secured the lease.

"Then she introduced me to everyone—one of whom was Connie who sells home stuff—and I went to my space to see how I wanted to decorate it. Max was there, and I asked her where I might find some furniture that would fit with the overall theme of the building, and Max said I should ask Connie."

"So, you called Connie over?"

"Not really. She was walking by and heard her name."

"Ah, Connie could hear Max?" Grandpa asked.

"No. I'd repeated Connie's name—that's what she heard. That's when I told her Max had recommended I check with her about where to find furniture. But Connie couldn't see her and said she didn't know anyone named Max. After Connie left, Max apologized and said she thought I knew she was a ghost."

"Do you still plan on leasing the shop?"

"Of course," I said. "Unless you think I shouldn't. I believe Max has had a hard life...or after...life, I guess. I believe it would be good for her to have me there."

"But is it good for you?"

"I don't think Max would harm me. She wasn't threatening in any way." I gave him a sharp look. "Do you feel she's only being nice to me until she gains my trust or something?"

"No." He blew out a breath. "Is this the first encounter you can remember having with...with the supernatural?"

"Yes."

For a few moments, the only sounds were those of the swing's chains clanging together, Grandpa Dave's rocker squeaking on the boards of the porch, and a bumble bee buzzing as it visited his red begonias.

At last, he broke the silence. "When you were a little girl, you sometimes saw people that no one else could see. Your parents thought you were making things up and scolded   you   until   you   either   stopped seeing...things....people...or you simply quit talking about it."

"They thought I was nuts," I said.

"No. Well, maybe. But they didn't understand you like I did."

"You mean, you see ghosts?"

"No, but my grandmother had the gift of...the sight—that's what she called it. She was kind of a spooky old bird, but she loved me and I loved her, and I didn't mind her eccentricities. I always believed you might've inherited her ability."

"Why didn't you tell me this before now?" I asked.

"I didn't see the need before. But now you've befriended a ghost, and you need to know you aren't crazy."

"Will you come back to the shop with me? I want to know if you can see her."

He grinned. "You need more reassurance you aren't insane, huh? Well, don't pin your hopes on this old man. I've never seen a ghost in my life."

"It's more than that." And it was...kinda. "I want you to help me pick out furniture."

"And you don't think I have anything better to do than that?"

"I know you do," I said. "But I'm your granddaughter."

We took Grandpa Dave's blue pickup truck back to Shops on Main. When we walked inside, Connie's door was ajar. She was with a customer, but she waved to us. We waved back before unlocking the door and stepping into my shop.

Max was sitting on the windowsill where I'd left her. "Good to see you're back. I was afraid I might've scared you off."

I glanced over at Grandpa because I was about to tell him that Max was here and that she'd just spoken to me, but I could tell by his wide eyes and slack jaw that he could see and hear her too.

Max winked at him. "Who's the silver fox? Got that expression from the old jewelry gal upstairs. It suits, though. You're a looker, mister."

Grandpa blinked a few times and extended his hand. "I'm Dave Tucker. You must be Max."

Max gave a tinkling laugh. "Darling, I wish I could shake your hand. I wanted to hug Amanda earlier, but I couldn't do that either."

"Grandpa, how can you see her?" I asked.

"The same way you can, I suppose."

"But you said you'd never seen a—" I glanced at the door to make sure we weren't being overheard. "—a ghost in your life."

"Max is my first."

Max placed a hand over her heart. "You make me blush, Dave. I haven't been anyone's first in ages." She laughed again, and he laughed with her.

I merely looked back and forth between them bewildered.

"Why are you surprised that I can see and talk with her?" Grandpa asked me. "You can."

"But no one else here can."

"That's true," Max said. "Maybe I'm special to the Tuckers. We'll have to look into it." She tilted her chin. "The love of my life was a Channing. Are there any Channings in your family?"

"My grandfather on my mother's side," said Grandpa Dave.

"Wasn't George, was it?"

"Yes." Grandpa's normally robust voice sounded very small and quiet.

Max got tears in her eyes. "I was running late to meet him the night I fell down the stairs...and died."

"I'm so sorry," Grandpa whispered.

Okay, this whole ghost thing was getting weirder by the second. Was it actually possible that Max had dated my great-great-grandfather?

I hated to ruin a strange but sappy moment. All right, no, I didn't hate to ruin this uncomfortable moment at all.

"So, hey, what do you think about having a small table in front of this window with chairs on either side?" I asked.

They both took the hint, and we started talking about decorating.

Grandpa and I had gone all over Abingdon, Bristol, and even Lebanon, but we'd managed to find some beautiful furniture and accessories for Designs on You. We had also talked on and off all afternoon about how strange it was that both he and I could see Max.

I hurried to the shop the next morning to await the delivery of the round table and upholstered chairs we'd bought to go in the sitting and fitting room.

I noticed there was some commotion on the street. There were police cars in front of Shops on Main, and one officer was directing traffic around an ambulance. I thought there must've been a car accident. I took the road leading to the back of the shop, so I couldn't see exactly what had happened. I parked in the lot and went inside through the back door.

An officer was there, and Frank and Ella were too.

"What's wrong?" I asked.

"It's Mark," said Ella. "He's dead."

"Mark…" I echoed.

"He's the web designer," Frank supplied.

"Of course. I met him yesterday. What happened to him? Was it a car accident?"

"Someone shot him," said Ella, "right in his office."

"It was actually right in his chest," said Max.

Chapter Three

I managed to ignore Max. "Who shot Mark?"

"Nobody knows," said Ella. "Mrs. Meacham found him when she came in this morning."

"He must've been killed last night," Frank said, rolling his eyes up to the ceiling as if he could see through the floorboards.

"We need to stop standing around speculating."

I turned to see Mrs. Meacham approaching us. It was obvious she'd been crying. I felt I—or someone—should put an arm around her, but I barely knew the woman.

"Everyone needs to lock up their space and leave," she said. "I have all the keys and will stay behind with the police as they go through your shops."

Ella gasped. "Go through our shop! Like we're common criminals? I won't have it!"

"You have no choice." Mrs. Meacham drew herself up to her full five and a half feet and raised her chin. "Shops on Main has been declared a crime scene, and the entire building is at the investigators' disposal. Furthermore, you will not return until the detectives give the all-clear."

Gayle Leeson

I looked at Max, who was standing by the door with her hands on her hips.

"Did you see who did this?" I asked her.

"No, dear," Mrs. Meacham said, patting me on the arm. "No one saw what happened."

"Neither did I," Max said. "I'm not omnipresent, you know."

I merely nodded. "I don't really have anything in my shop yet except for a few pieces of furniture, and I haven't unlocked the door this morning. Please let me know if you need me for anything, Mrs. Meacham."

"I will, dear." She gave Ella a pointed look. "Thank you for your understanding and cooperation."

"I'll keep an eye on the investigation and let you know what I hear," Max said. "Don't worry."

"It's hard not to worry," I said.

"I know it's distressing," Mrs. Meacham said. "This is a terrible thing to have happened. Should I call someone to come and pick you up?"

"No. No, I'll be all right. Thank you."

An authoritative male voice called from upstairs. "Mrs. Meacham, we need you up here."

"I have to go," she said. "Are you sure I can't call anyone for you, Amanda?"

"No, thank you. I'm fine."

"She's made of sterner stuff than you give her credit for," Max declared, giving her head a shake that set her bob to bouncing.

I gave Max a wan smile, and she winked. "See you soon! I'm off to see what the coppers have found." And then she was gone.

Grandpa Dave had been waiting for me to call about getting the rest of the furniture moved into the shop today. I called him as soon as I got into the car and told him what happened.

"Oh, Pup, that's awful! Are you all right?"

"I'm fine." I fully considered the magnitude of the situation for the first time. "Poor Mark. I wonder if this was a random thing or if he was murdered by someone who knew him?"

"Either way, if you've changed your mind and no longer want to open your shop, I'm sure Mrs. Meacham will understand and will refund your deposit."

"N-no. I don't want to make any rash decisions." I happened to consider that my opening a shop was a rash decision. "Or, you know, any *more* rash decisions. I'm going to wait and see what the detectives find."

"They won't give out any information," Grandpa said.

"No, but Max will."

"Did you see her this morning?"

"I did, but she didn't witness the murder or anything."

He blew out a breath. "How about I come get you and take you to Luke's for lunch in a couple of hours?"

"That'd be nice, Grandpa."

"Are you sure you're okay, Pup?"

"I'm a little shook up, but I'm fine. By the way, would you mind calling the furniture store where we got the table and chairs and making other arrangements? They were supposed to be delivered this morning."

"I'll take care of it."

When I got home, I went into the living room, sank onto the tan overstuffed sofa, and cuddled Jazzy onto my lap. I picked up my tablet and clicked on the web browser. I thought I could maybe get my mind off Mark and his murder by seeing if I could find anything about Max online. After all, lots of newspapers had their archives on the Internet.

I checked the *Abingdon Virginian* since it was the premier newspaper in Abingdon for over a hundred and fifty years. The Library of Congress had archives dating from 1849 to 1901. And, fortunately, former editor and publisher Robert Weisfeld had archived the newspaper from 1900 to 2006—the year the newspaper shut down—on a private site that included a tribute to his mother Martha, who had helmed the paper prior to her retirement.

In searching for Maxine Englebright, I discovered that my friendly neighborhood ghost had been quite the socialite. That didn't really surprise me even with the limited knowledge I had of her. I found a photo of Max sporting her freshly-cut bob outside a local salon, much to the apparent disapproval of her mother, who was standing off to the side, arms crossed, glaring at her daughter. I saved the photo to show Max.

There was also a photo of Max in the midst of a group of women fervently supporting the ratification of the Nineteenth Amendment in 1920, which gave women the right to vote. Max was wearing a cloche hat and a darling skirt suit, and she was holding a glass of champagne aloft as she smiled at the camera. I leaned in closer. All the women at the rally had champagne.

Hmm…must've been before Prohibition.

I saved that photo to my tablet too. I thought Max might get a kick out of seeing herself.

Another article was dated after Max's death but gave the sad news that the Englebright home was sold in 1931 after the family finally succumbed to bankruptcy from the stock market crash of 1929. I wouldn't share that information with Max. If she wasn't aware of her family's financial struggle after her death, I didn't want to be the bearer of bad news.

At Luke's Café, Grandpa Dave and I settled in at our favorite table beneath a collection of Marilyn Monroe photographs. The waitress brought us menus, but we didn't need them. I ordered the chicken salad croissant with homemade chips and a side of fruit, and Grandpa ordered the club sandwich with fries. We waited until the waitress had delivered our drinks—sodas in mason jar glasses—before discussing what had happened this morning at Shops on Main.

I kept my voice just above a whisper. "When I got there, I thought there might have been an accident or something….you know, because of all the police cars. But then I went inside, and Frank and Ella told me that Mark was shot in his office. Max said it was in the chest."

People at a table near ours were also speaking in hushed tones, and I thought it was likely they were also talking about the murder. It would be foremost in just about everybody's mind today.

Grandpa nodded. "But Max didn't see who did it? Doesn't know who might've done it?"

"Apparently not. And even if she did, what could I do with that information? I couldn't very well go to the police and say, 'My ghost friend Max said this is the person who killed Mark.'"

"Well, no." He sipped his soda. "You say she was going to linger near the investigators to see what she can learn?"

"That's what she told me."

"Hopefully, then, she can at least tell you whether or not they believe it was a random act or the work of someone with a grudge against the man. Either way, I don't want you in the place by yourself."

"I won't be."

He raised an index finger. "I know how you get when you're caught up in your work. You lose track of everything."

"I know, but I'll be careful." I lowered my eyes to the colorfully painted table. "I won't be in the building alone."

"All right."

Eager to push aside the thought that it might be dangerous to work in Shops on Main alone, I pulled out my tablet and located the images I'd saved. "Check out these photos I found of Max."

Grandpa chuckled. "She was a feisty girl, wasn't she?"

"Was? I believe she still is."

"You're right."

"I'm going to show these to her when I go back to the shop." I returned the tablet to my purse. "By the way, would you mind helping me design a logo for Designs on You?"

"Designs on You? That's what you're calling your shop?"

I nodded.

"I like it!"

The waitress returned with our food, and Grandpa Dave proudly announced that I was the new proprietress of Designs on You, a fashion boutique that would be opening up at the first of the month.

"Wow! Where will you be located?"

"Sh—" I stopped myself just in the nick of time. I didn't want to mention Shops on Main today. "Main street. I'll bring in a flyer when I'm a little closer to being ready to open."

"Great! I'll look forward to it." She nodded toward our plates. "Is there anything else I can bring you?"

We both said no, and as she walked away, I cut my croissant in half.

"Sorry. I kinda jumped the gun there," said Grandpa.

"No, you didn't. But I didn't want to tell her the…well, the exact location…not today."

"Good thinking."

Grandpa Dave has a terrific eye, so when we went back to my house, we both sat down with sketch pads and started doodling ideas for the Designs on You logo. Naturally, Grandpa came up with the perfect logo. It was an evening gown on a dressmaker's mannequin—navy blue with a lighter blue accent across the shoulders and a slit up the right side—and *Designs on You* written in an elegant font.

"I love it!" I said.

"Let's see what you came up with," he said.

I turned my blank page toward him, and we both laughed.

"So now what?"

"Now we order all the stuff." I hurried to my bedroom to retrieve my laptop and smiled to myself when I heard him telling Jazzy he had no idea what all the stuff was.

When I returned to the living room, and after I'd scanned his logo into the computer, I sat beside him on the sofa and showed him: business cards, postcards, garment bags, invoices, envelopes, a door sign, and a window decal. I also ordered one more dress form and a mannequin.

"I already have two dress forms," I explained to Grandpa, "but I know I'll need more. And I'll want to be able to keep one at home for when I'm working here."

"I understand."

"And I'm also going to need another machine for the shop."

He raised his brows. "I see why you needed so much start-up cash."

I laughed. "It really is a loan."

He waved off my assertion with a flick of his wrist, but I was determined to pay him back. I only hoped the business was successful enough to allow me to do so within a reasonable amount of time.

"All right...do we need to go shopping for a sewing machine then?" he asked.

"Aw...I wouldn't ask you to do that, Grandpa."

"I'd be happy to."

He simply didn't want me to be alone today, and we both knew it. As a matter of fact, I didn't want me to be alone either.

"Okay, let's do it. And, afterward, we'll come back here and I'll make us some dinner."

"And we could watch a movie," he suggested.

I smiled and hugged him. It was nice to have someone looking out for me.

Grandpa and I did go and get another sewing machine along with a sewing table. We left both in the trunk of my car so I could take them inside when I returned to Shops on Main. I had to admit it would be a little spooky going back in now that I knew someone had been murdered there. I mean, Max had died there, but her death had been an accident.

As we drove, I mentioned that I didn't have many items for my *prête a porter*—or ready-to-wear—line. I had a sample of several garments I'd made for myself, but that was it.

"Hadn't you better remedy that?" Grandpa asked.

"Yes, I guess I'd better. Would you mind a quick stop by the fabric store?"

"Not at all. I'm at your disposal today."

Despite the fact that I'd never made a "quick" stop by the fabric store in my life, I decided I'd do my best not to linger today. As I perused the bolts of jersey fabric, a royal blue caught my eye. It brought to mind a dress I'd sketched with an A-line skirt and lace cap sleeves. I'd made the dress blue with a black-and-white polka dot

Gayle Leeson

panel insert on the skirt. I placed the blue in my cart and searched for the polka dot fabric. When I found it, I let out a whoop of delight.

"Do I want to know?" Grandpa asked.

"You'll see," I told him. "I'm going to make a dress using these two fabrics in five sizes and have it available to customers when the shop opens."

He turned his mouth down. "All righty."

Grandpa was right to be a little skeptical. I was supposed to open the shop in a week. But this would be an easy dress to make, and I was confident I could make five by the time I opened the shop.

"You know, we should do some sort of open house before you actually open to the public...invite the press...that sort of thing."

"Normally, I'd think that was a great idea, Grandpa. But after what happened to Mark, I think it would be best to wait until later to throw a party."

"You're right. I wasn't thinking."

I kissed his cheek and then went off to find a bolt of lace that would match my royal blue fabric.

As Grandpa and I were headed back home at last, my phone rang. I didn't recognize the number, but I answered it anyway using the car's built-in Bluetooth device.

"Hello, dear. It's Melba Meacham."

"Hi, Mrs. Meacham. How are you?"

"I'm fine. How are you? You seemed to be quite upset when you left this morning."

"Yes, well…it was a terrible shock."

"Indeed it was. But the police have told me that tomorrow morning, they will be out of the building and we may reenter. You are still planning on taking the space, aren't you?"

"Of course, I am."

"Good. I thought the…uh…what transpired… might have made you change your mind."

"No, I'm still planning to open the shop at the first of the month. As a matter of fact, I've ordered all my supplies and picked up an additional sewing machine."

"Marvelous! I'm happy to hear it."

"Did…did the police tell you anything else?" I asked.

"Only that someone would be moving all of Mark's things out of his office either tomorrow or the next day."

"Things…like his client files?"

"I imagine they took those and Mark's computer already," said Mrs. Meacham. "I believe they were referring to having his family come in for his personal effects."

"Oh." The sound emerged small and a bit strangled, and Grandpa patted my shoulder just to remind me he was near. "Th-that's so sad."

"Yes. Well, dear, I have to finish contacting everyone to let them know it's business as usual tomorrow."

"Thank you for calling."

I ended the call and glanced at Grandpa. "Gee. Business as usual."

"Life does go on, Pup."

"I know. It just seems harsh. I'd only met the man one time, but he appeared to be nice enough. I feel so sorry for his family."

"I'm anxious to see what Max tells us the detectives found."

"Us?" I asked with a wry grin.

"Sure! There's no way you can move your furniture in tomorrow all alone."

Chapter Four

I was a little trepidatious returning to Shops on Main Thursday morning, and I was glad Grandpa Dave was right behind me in his truck when I pulled into the parking lot. I waited for him before going inside. It was a beautiful late summer morning. The sun was shining down through the leaves of the maple trees at the side of the parking lot, and a mourning dove called from somewhere overhead. It seemed an appropriate bird to be here this somber day.

"What do you want to start with?" I asked Grandpa.

"Let's start with the sewing tables," he said. "They're on wheels, and they'll be easier to move around once we decide where we want them."

The sewing tables and sewing machines were in my car, so I popped the trunk, put the keys in my pocket and grabbed a table. Grandpa Dave did the same, and we headed into the building. Luckily, he was ahead of me and was able to open the door.

When we got inside, we saw that the shop owners had gathered in the hallway between my shop and Connie's.

Gayle Leeson

"Is…is everything all right?" I asked, afraid of what the answer might be.

"We're all going to work together to make sure it is," Connie said. "I was just telling the others that I cleansed my shop, the kitchen, the bathrooms, and the hallways earlier this morning with sage."

That explains the smell.

"And I'll be happy to cleanse your shops too."

"What do you mean?" Janice asked, impatiently looking at her long red manicured nails.

"Burning sage drives out negative energies," Connie said. "There's a lot of anger, hurt, and, well, maybe even Mark's restless spirit in this house. Cleansing helps restore positive energy. And, if Mark's still here, it could help him go to the light."

Burning sage could send a spirit to the light? Max!

I didn't want Max to go to the light. But, then, that was selfish. I wanted what was best for her. Truly, I did. But I at least wanted to be able to tell her goodbye.

I hadn't realized I'd gasped until Connie came, took the sewing table out of my hands, placed it on the floor, and hugged me.

"There's nothing to be frightened about," she said. "Would you like me to cleanse your shop now?"

Grandpa said, "I'm sure she would as soon as we get this furniture moved in. Smoke bothers my sinuses."

It didn't really, but he knew me well enough to realize I was concerned about Max, and the smoke provided a good excuse for Connie not to burn sage in my shop just yet.

"All right." Connie smiled. "I haven't got any customers yet—people might even think we're closed today—so I'll be able to help with the furniture."

"Me too," said Ford.

"I can run upstairs and cleanse your shop while you men are grabbing some of the heavier items," Connie said.

"I appreciate the offer," he said, "but I have some sage. I'll take care of my shop and Mark's office...if it's open."

"Aw, that's great. Ella, would you and Frank like me to cleanse Everything Paper before I help with the furniture?"

"Nope," said Frank firmly. "I don't go in for that mumbo jumbo. But I'll help with the furniture."

"Thank you all for being so generous." I took my keys from my pocket and unlocked the door to my shop. I carried the sewing table inside, and Connie took the other one from Grandpa so the men could go on back out to the parking lot.

I glanced around the shop but didn't see Max. Was she still here? Or had Connie saged her away?

Forty minutes later—and still no sign of Max—everyone else had gone back to their shops, and Grandpa Dave and I were arranging the furniture. I had a small writing desk and chair, two sewing machines on sewing tables, chairs to be placed in front of each of those machines, two navy blue wingback chairs to be placed on either side of the front window with a small round marble table between them, two dress forms, two full mannequins, a three-way, full-length mirror, and an Oriental privacy screen for measurements and fittings.

Grandpa was standing in the middle of the room with his hands on his hips surveying the room.

"Do you think she's gone?" I asked quietly.

"Hmm?" He was distracted. "Would Mrs. Meacham let me build some shelves in here, or does everything have to be removable?"

"I don't know. We can ask." I turned in a full circle, not appreciating the beauty of my new shop as Grandpa apparently thought, but still looking for Max.

He came over and put an arm around my neck. "It's looking good, Pup. I'm proud of you."

"Me too!"

I gasped and spun around to see Max standing behind us. I put my arms out to hug her, remembered that I couldn't, and hugged Grandpa instead. "She's still here!"

"Did you think I wasn't?" she asked.

"I was afraid Connie saged you away," I said softly. "She's been burning the stuff all throughout the building."

Max shrugged. "Didn't bother me."

"Well, we're glad it didn't," Grandpa said. "So…you like what we've done with the place? I know we still have a lot to do, but—"

"I love it." Max smiled at me. "You've outdone yourself. Both of you." She tilted her head at the mannequins. "I will be glad when you put some clothes on those poor things, though."

"That's the next trip. I've got samples to put on the mannequins, and I'm working on a dress for the *prête-a-porter* line."

"Fantastic!" She turned to Grandpa. "And what's this about you building shelves, Silver Fox? Are you a carpenter?"

"I piddle," he said.

"He builds some of the most beautiful things ever," I told her.

"What did you learn from spying on the police?" he asked Max.

"Well, the detectives were extremely interested in Mark's client files and his ledgers. It makes sense that it might be a disgruntled customer. Mrs. Meacham told them that Mark had been having trouble paying his rent and that he was leaving at the end of this month."

"That's right," I said. "She mentioned that to me too. Do you think it's possible Mark was killed because of his debts?"

"I doubt it, Pup. That sort of thing happens on television and in the movies, but I don't think it happens that often in real life. Dead men don't pay their debts."

"Excellent point," Max said. "After Mrs. Meacham left, the detectives speculated about where all Mark's money could be going, if indeed he had any. Either business was bad, or else there was something else Mark was spending all his money on—a girlfriend, drugs, something like that."

"Was Mark married?" I asked.

"I don't believe so," Max said. "He didn't keep any photographs on his desk."

"Did you see a lot of customers visiting him here?" Grandpa Dave asked.

"No…but then I didn't give it much thought. I wasn't very interested in his work."

"At least, at this point, it doesn't appear the police think this murder was random," Grandpa said. "That's a relief. It's bad enough to know there's a killer out there. Much worse to think he's targeting anyone and everyone."

I took my tablet from my purse and sat on one of the wingback chairs. "Let's take a break before we move the rest of this furniture into place."

"All right." Grandpa pulled the other navy chair beside me and sat down. "This is more comfortable that I thought it would be."

After turning on the tablet, I pulled up the first of the photos I'd gotten from the *Abingdon Virginian*. It was the one of Max standing outside the salon. "Remember this?"

Max laughed. "I do! Mother was scandalized that I'd had my hair bobbed. I was the first gal in town to do it. Oh, look at how disgusted she was." She laughed again. "I miss that old grouch."

I swiped that photo away, and the image of the ratification rally came up.

"How'd you do that?" she asked.

I moved my finger across the screen, and the salon photo returned.

"May I try it?" After my nod, Max waved her hand over the screen, and the rally photo filled the screen. She squealed in delight. "I did it! I turned the pages of the photo album."

"How did you get away with drinking champagne during Prohibition?" Grandpa asked.

"Oh, darling, it wasn't illegal to drink during Prohibition…just to make, sell, or transport the stuff."

"I remember your saying that you loved to read," I murmured.

"I do…did." She shrugged.

I opened the e-reader application and opened *Speedy Death* by Gladys Mitchell. "This one was originally published in 1929. I downloaded it for you last night. I thought—"

"A book? You got me a book? And I can read it on there? This is wonderful! Thank you!"

"Since you're able to swipe the pages, you can read while Grandpa and I move furniture."

She merely nodded, eager to begin. I placed the tablet on the small marble table and then moved the table near the window.

"Is that okay? Or does it cause a glare?" I asked.

"It's fine." She was already devouring the book.

Grandpa and I shared a smile. I felt slightly selfish about it, but I was glad Max was still here. And she must be happy about it too, or else, she'd have left.

By the time Max was halfway through her book, Grandpa Dave and I had turned the shop into Designs on You.

I beamed at him. "It's beautiful!"

The two wingback chairs were angled toward the small marble table that sat in front of the window. My writing desk was directly across the room from the door, so it—and, most likely I—would be the first thing clients would see when they walked into the shop. A dress form with the first completed royal blue dress with the black-and-white polka dot accent from my prete-a-porter line stood in one corner, and a mannequin wearing the custom 1930s-style red evening gown stood in the other.

The Oriental privacy screen stood just inside the workshop, or the atelier. This was where I'd put the shelving Grandpa Dave was going to make for my fabric. Mrs. Meacham had told him he couldn't anchor anything to the walls but that he could make as many free-standing shelves as he'd like. I knew he'd make something sturdy but also lovely. The atelier was also where I'd placed my sewing machines, a long white table for cutting fabric, a tall metal filing cabinet to house my patterns, a full-length three-way mirror, and the two other mannequins.

Grandpa surveyed both rooms, and I could tell he was happy with our handiwork. "I do see one thing you're missing, though."

"What's that?"

"A rolling clothes rack. You're going to need one—maybe two—for that porta-potty line."

I laughed. "*Prête-a-porter*. Let's just call it ready-to-wear. And, you're right. I entirely forgot about that."

"Why don't I run out and see what I can find and grab us a bite of lunch?"

"I can go too," I said.

"Nonsense. Stay here and talk books with Max…that is, if you can tear her away from the one she's reading."

"I heard that," she said dryly. "Forgive me for tuning you out, darlings. It's just been so very long since I've had any good books to read."

Grandpa kissed my cheek. "I'll be back in a jiffy."

"Thank you."

He left, closing the door behind him, but I could hear him asking Connie, Ella, and Frank if they'd like him to pick them up anything while he was out.

Max tilted her head. She was listening as well…and obviously had excellent hearing.

"Hmm…Frank's going with him," she said.

"Frank's going with Grandpa Dave?"

She nodded. "I suppose he's delighted to have some male company. He's the sore thumb down here, and the men upstairs have always kept to themselves."

"Doesn't he need to stay here and help Ella watch the store?"

"No. From the way she acts, he's usually just in her way."

"Aw…that's sad."

Max shrugged. "I'm not saying she's a harpy or anything…only that she's a perfectionist—at least, where that shop is concerned—and she wants everything done a certain way. It's usually best for Frank if he sits back and lets her do it all."

"And then does she complain about having to do everything?" I asked.

"Of course."

We laughed.

"It's wonderful having you here," Max said. "And thank you for showing me how to use your book computer."

"I'll have you watching videos next."

"Videos? You mean, like the movies?"

Before I could answer, there was an uproar out in the hallway. I raced to the door and flung it open. There was a tall, gaunt woman with long black hair standing in the foyer weeping.

Connie had gotten to the woman already and was soothing her. Ella was standing nearby wringing her hands and looking from side to side. Mrs. Meacham was hurrying down the steps.

"Mrs. Meacham, this is Lorinda, Mark's mother," Connie said.

"Oh…" Mrs. Meacham went to Lorinda's side and patted her shoulder awkwardly. "Oh…we're…we're all so sorry for your loss, Ms. Tinsley."

Tinsley…I hadn't known Mark's surname until now.

"Why don't you come on into my shop and have a seat?" Connie suggested.

"No. No…" She gazed around the foyer. "I need to be right here. I feel a supernatural presence here."

Max, who'd come to stand beside me, raised a hand and wiggled her fingers in greeting. I looked wide-eyed from her to Lorinda Tinsley and back again.

"I have a strong sixth sense," Ms. Tinsley continued, "and I feel Mark's presence here." She looked toward the ceiling. "Mark, my sweet, I'm here for you."

Connie also looked around above all our heads and offered, "We're all here, Mark. We're so terribly sorry for what happened to you."

"We're going to see that you get justice, son." Ms. Tinsley turned to Connie. "We need to have a séance here so that Mark may reveal to us the identity of his killer."

"I'm afraid we…" It was obvious—to me, at least— that Mrs. Meacham was grappling for a plausible excuse. "We aren't zoned for…for séances. And, besides, Ms. Tinsley, I must appeal to your sense of privacy. Would you really want rubberneckers coming here to see where Mark… well, you know?"

"I want to bring my son's killer to justice, no matter what it takes."

"You could have the séance at my house," Connie said. "The children will be at school tomorrow from eight a.m. until two-thirty p.m. I'll close the shop for an hour and meet you at my house for the…the ceremony…if you think it would help."

Ms. Tinsley sighed. "It would be better to do it here—in Mark's office even." She turned a bitter glare in Mrs. Meacham's direction. "But if that's not possible, then, yes, I'd appreciate that."

"Any of you who'd like to participate are welcome to join us," Connie said.

"I appreciate the offer, but I need to be here running the shop," Ella said. "In fact, I'd better get back." She quickly hurried into the haven of Everything Paper.

"I'll come," I said.

"Fantastic." Connie smiled. "I'll give you the address later. Ms. Tinsley, if you'll come with me, I'll give you directions to my house."

As Connie and Ms. Tinsley walked into Delightful Home, Mrs. Meacham shook her head. "I don't know if I'd be getting involved with that, if I were you."

"I'd just like to be helpful…if possible. Everyone has been so kind to me."

"Yes, well… That woman should allow her son to rest in peace." She trudged back up the stairs.

I walked back into Designs on You and realized Max was already there. "But what if he can't?"

"Can't what?" she asked.

"What if Mark can't rest in peace?"

"I think he is." She shrugged. "His spirit didn't hang around here."

"Really?"

"Really. Or, at least, I haven't seen him. I'm not sure how this ghost thing works for everyone else, but I've never seen another one. And, I've been in this house when other people died, but I've never encountered the deceased person's spirit."

"Why do you think it is that you haven't moved on, Max?"

"I don't know that either." She grinned. "Maybe I've been hanging around here waiting to meet you and the silver fox."

When Grandpa and Frank returned with lunch, we went into the kitchen to eat. Ella and Frank sat on one side of the Formica table, and Grandpa and I sat on the other. The chairs were red vinyl, and I wondered if the set had been here for ages or if someone had bought them and refinished them recently.

"This retro dining set is in excellent shape," I observed.

Grandpa was agreeing with me, but Ella didn't have time to extol the virtues of a table and chairs. She flew right in to telling Frank—and thus, Grandpa and me, who already knew everything and was planning on telling Grandpa privately—about Mark's mother's visit.

"The woman wanted to have a séance! Can you believe that, Frank? A séance—right here in this very house...more precisely, in Mark's old office. She wants to conjure him up and ask who killed him."

"That's kind of gruesome, if you ask me," Frank said. "Is she really going to do it?"

"Not here. Mrs. Meacham put her foot down and said no indeedy." Ella gave a nod to punctuate her fictional word. "But you know Connie. She's into all of that weird stuff, and she told Mark's mother that she could have the séance at her place while her kids were in school."

Grandpa's eyes shifted to me, and I raised and lowered one shoulder. Hopefully, I conveyed to him that I didn't want to discuss Mark's mother or séances right now but preferred eating my lunch.

"Connie asked if I'd like to come, and I told her I needed to stay here and watch the shop," Ella continued. "She was able to rope poor Amanda into it, though."

"Honey, you don't have to do everything these people tell you to do," Frank said to me. "Connie is a nice woman and all, but she has some peculiar notions."

I studied on my answer. I didn't want to alienate the Petermans when I was just getting to know them. But I also didn't want to be unfriendly to Connie. I had nothing pressing to do tomorrow since my shop didn't actually open until Monday, and I wanted to attend this séance. I'd never tried to communicate with the dead—well, other than Max, and I felt she was exceptional—and I'd like to see what it was all about. Besides, if I could help catch Mark's killer, that would be wonderful...and we'd all rest easier.

Frank apparently took my silence as shyness and changed the subject to something he'd seen in the hardware store.

Once Grandpa Dave and I were alone in Designs on You, I mentioned to him that Max didn't think Mark's spirit was here.

"I agree with Frank about your not going along with whatever these people suggest, Pup. Not because you're going to this séance, but because one of the people at Shops on Main might have killed Mark Tinsley."

Chapter Five

Grandpa had left over an hour ago to begin work on the shelves, and I'd stayed behind to give the place a final check. Honestly, I think I was mainly waiting around to see if Max would show up again. I hadn't seen her since lunch. But I realized I needed to get home too. I still had four dresses to make before Monday, and I was giving up part of my day tomorrow for the séance.

I left my tablet on the writing desk, retrieved my purse from the atelier, and made sure the door that led into the kitchen was locked. Then I left through the front door, locked it, and took a step backward.

When I stepped back, I ran into something large and solid, and I felt myself falling. In a panic, I flailed my arms out to my sides. Two strong arms came around me and pulled me upright. I gripped one of those arms as if it were a lifeline.

"Th-thank you." I looked up into one of the most gorgeous faces I'd ever seen in my life. A pair of light blue eyes, a strong jawline, beautiful teeth… "Goodness." The word escaped my lips before I'd realized it.

"I'll say!"

Of all times for Max to show back up…

"Good job!" she enthused.

"I didn't trip on purpose!" I protested.

Mr. Gorgeous laughed. "I never thought you did."

"Right," I said. "I'm…I'm just…kinda clumsy, and…"

"Hush before he decides you're an idiot," Max said. "He thinks you're adorable. Don't blow it."

I opened my mouth to speak, but then I shut it again. Whether Max was right about this man thinking I was adorable or not, she was certainly correct in her assertion that he would believe me to be an idiot.

After more carefully weighing my words, I simply said, "I'm sorry."

"Actually, I'm glad we bumped into each other." He smiled. "I'm not glad I nearly tripped you—and I sincerely apologize for that—but since we'll be working together, it's nice to meet you. I'm Jason Logan."

I realized Jason Logan was still holding me against his hard chest, and I was still gripping his arm. I took a step back.

"What'd you do that for?" Max grumbled.

Holding out my hand, I said, "I'm Amanda Tucker."

Jason and I shook hands.

"You're opening the cigar shop?"

"No, luckily for me, that deal fell through. I'm a professional photographer, and I've leased an office upstairs." He twisted his lips in a wry grimace. "At least, I think I have. It's the office that belonged to Mark Tinsley. I need to go up and check with Mrs. Meacham to see if it's still all right for me to start on Monday or if I need to look for another office."

"Oh... I hope..." I struggled to find the words that would convey what I wanted to say without sounding like I desperately wanted us to be working in the same building. Because I desperately wanted us to be working in the same building. "I hope everything will be all right...you know, with the office."

"Me too."

"Um...you won't be creeped out working where someone was murdered?" I asked.

Jason smiled. "I might be. Would it be okay if I come visit your shop whenever things get too creepy upstairs?"

"Anytime!" Max said.

"Anytime," I parroted.

"Great. What do you do, Amanda?"

"I'm a fashion designer...and I'm new here too. I just got everything moved in today."

"May I see your shop?"

"Of course." I stepped over to the door, unlocked it, and ushered him inside.

"This is terrific!" Jason walked around the front room before walking into the atelier. "Have you ever modeled?"

"Who? Me? No."

"Oh, but you could, darling," said Max. "He's going to make an offer, or else he wouldn't have mentioned it. Take him up on it."

"You should let me take some photos of you in some of the clothes you've designed," Jason said. "You could put them on your walls."

"Th-that would be…nice, but I'm…I'm not sure I can afford it." Besides, I was not model material. When I thought of models, I thought of those girls who were all angles and frowns walking the runways.

"I'll do it for free," he said. "It'll be terrific publicity for me when your clients see my work."

"I don't have any clients yet."

"But you will." He placed his hands on my shoulders. "What do you say?"

Max sighed. "Say yes to anything he wants."

"Yes," I said. Darn it! Max and I needed to have a talk about her interference! "I…I think some photographs would be great."

"Good. Maybe we can set it up for Saturday."

Before I could respond, Mrs. Meacham walked through the door. "Jason, good, I thought I heard your voice. I was going to call you, and now I don't have to. The cleaners will be in tomorrow to…um…you know, finish tidying the space, and Monday, the office will be all yours."

"Thank you, Mrs. Meacham. Are you sure you don't need more time to clear everything out? I'm fine waiting, as long as it's not too long."

"Oh, no, no. Everything will be shipshape for you on Monday." She smiled at me. "I'm glad you two are getting to know each other. A fashionista and a photographer seem to go hand in hand."

Mrs. Meacham left, and Jason turned to me. "She's right. So, about Saturday. Would you like to meet here at ten a.m.?"

"Ten is good. I'll see you then."

I ignored pretending-to-swoon Max as I left the shop and locked the door.

When I got home, I sat on the sofa, kicked off my shoes, and stretched out to think about Jason Logan. He was probably dating someone. Someone that hot couldn't be single. I wished I hadn't been so eager to take him up on his offer of a free photo shoot. But Mrs. Meacham was right—fashion and photography did go hand in hand. And the photographs could benefit Jason's business as well as mine. Cross-promotion is always a good thing.

Jazzy came and pounced onto my stomach. I stroked her chin, and she began to purr.

"Once I get settled in, I'd like to take you to the shop with me," I told her.

She was extra attentive because she wanted to be fed. I kissed the top of her head, placed her on the floor and stood. She followed me into the kitchen where I put a can of food into her dish and refilled her water bowl.

"I'm going to a séance tomorrow," I said.

Jazzy didn't even bother to look up from her food.

"I don't know what the protocol is for something like that. I am going to Connie's home, so I should take some sort of hostess gift…right?"

Standing on my tiptoes, I took my recipe box from the top shelf. I found a recipe for coffee cake that looked good. And coffee cake seemed like an acceptable hostess gift, séance or not.

As I took out my metal mixing bowl and began combining the ingredients, I wondered who else would be at the séance. Mark's mother, for sure. Ella and Mrs. Meacham would definitely not be there. What about Janice?

I frowned as it occurred to me that I hadn't seen Janice all day. Had she stayed at home, or had she merely been upstairs staying under the radar? That didn't seem likely. Even though I'd only been at Shops on Main for a couple of days—and in and out then—it appeared to me that

Janice made herself seen and heard when she was there. So where had she been? I made a mental note to ask Connie tomorrow morning.

The next morning, I fed Jazzy, ate some toast, and headed off to Connie's house. Connie lived about halfway between Abingdon and Winter Garden, Virginia. I passed the Down South Café on my way and thought Grandpa Dave and I should go there for lunch again soon.

I was the first to arrive and told Connie I hoped I wasn't too early. She assured me it was fine as she graciously accepted the coffee cake.

"Have you had breakfast, Amanda?"

"Yes. But go ahead and have some of the cake, if you'd like."

"Oh, no," said Connie. "I had breakfast with my children. If it's all right with you, I'll save the cake for later."

"That's fine. I just didn't want to visit your house for the first time without bringing a hostess gift." For the first time? Did that sound bad? Will Connie think I now expect to be invited to visit her on a regular basis? Maybe I should clarify.

Before I could elaborate, Connie praised my strong sense of Southern hospitality. "Did your mom teach you that?"

"No. My Grandma Jodie did. She was a stickler for good manners."

"She's your Grandpa Dave's wife?"

"She was, yes. She passed on about five years ago." I realized I was here to attend a séance, so I added, "Not that I want to communicate with her today or anything. I miss her, and I'd like to say hello, but not today. This is Mark's day."

Connie laughed. "You're ever so thoughtful."

"Thank you." I looked around Connie's country chic home. There were lots of distressed white tables and cabinets. A matching overstuffed sofa, love seat and chair were covered in colorful afghans and throw pillows. There was a large braided rug in the center of the floor, and some branches stood in a vase on a table near the front window. Plus, the room smelled like lemon, thanks to the aromatherapy diffuser that shared the table with the vase. "You have a beautiful place here."

"I appreciate that. Have you ever attended a séance before, Amanda?"

"I haven't. Have you?"

"Once or twice. It's been awhile though. I do believe that we can't even begin to comprehend the mysteries of the universe, so I keep an open mind."

The doorbell sounded, and Connie went to admit Lorinda. She brought the woman back into the living room where I'd perched on the armchair.

"Lorinda, this is Amanda Tucker. Amanda, this is Lorinda—Mark's mother."

I rose and shook Lorinda's hand. "I'm so very sorry for your loss. I saw you yesterday at Shops on Main, but we didn't actually meet. So, it's nice to make your acquaintance...I only wish it was under different circumstances."

"As do I, dear." Lorinda smiled. "You're quite lovely."

"Um...thank you." I always felt awkward when I received a compliment.

"You *are* the young woman Mark was seeing...aren't you?" Lorinda asked.

My eyes flew to Connie's just as she dropped hers to the floor.

"No. I'm sorry...I'd only met Mark once. My shop doesn't open until Monday."

"Oh...I see," said Lorinda. "Then who--?"

Connie appeared to be relieved when the doorbell rang again. I gave Lorinda a tight smile and wondered who Mark had dated at Shops on Main. It must've been whoever was leasing the retail space Designs on You now occupied, since I couldn't imagine him dating anyone I'd met there. Or maybe Mark's mother was always harping on him about settling down, and he'd invented a girlfriend to get her off his back.

Connie returned with Sabine, the psychic, a plump woman with auburn hair and dark eyes. Sabine wore a black t-shirt dress with a turquoise pendant, matching hoop earrings, and rings on every finger of her left hand.

We all moved into the dining room. The distressed white furniture theme had carried over into this room as well, and there were navy and white checked cushions on the chair seats. Sabine took a large pillar candle from her tote and placed it in the center of the table.

"Is this all of us?" I asked Connie.

She nodded.

"Hmm...I thought maybe Janice would be joining us."

Connie's eyes widened. "No, she won't be here." She hurried to see if there was anything Sabine needed.

The table was rectangular and sat six, so we arranged ourselves on the four chairs in the middle. Lorinda and Sabine sat on one side of the table, and Connie and I sat directly across from them. Sabine lit the candle, and we all joined hands. I held hands with Connie and Lorinda. I was nervous and hoped my palms weren't sweaty.

Sabine began to speak. "Mark...we're here for you, Mark. We're all here for you. Let's speak our names so he knows who we are."

She nodded for Connie to begin, but Lorinda wasn't taking any chances.

"Mark, it's me, your mother. Connie, Sabine, and Amanda are here too. I love you so much." She choked on the words. "I'm sorry you're gone. I hate that you died such a violent death, but I'm going to avenge you, my sweet boy. I miss you terribly."

Tears ran unchecked down Lorinda's cheeks, and I got a bit teary myself. I'd only met Mark once, but I could certainly commiserate with a woman who'd lost someone she loved so dearly. I glanced at Connie and saw tears glistening on her cheeks as well. Only Sabine was completely focused on the task at hand.

"Be quiet now," she told Lorinda softly. "Don't overwhelm him. We need to give him a moment to come through."

We were all silent for several seconds, and then Sabine tried once again to summon Mark. As a matter of fact, she tried a few times—and Lorinda jumped in there and helped a time or two—but no luck. Mark Tinsley didn't make an appearance.

"Maybe it's good that he's not here," Connie suggested. "Maybe that means he's moved on and is at peace."

"It didn't work because Mark's spirit isn't in this house," Lorinda said. "He's there where his office was. And I'm going to find out whether that zoning excuse

Melba Meacham gave me is a real thing or not. If it isn't, Sabine and I will most certainly be communicating with Mark there."

Soon after that declaration, Lorinda and Sabine left.

Connie looked at me and asked, "I'd like a piece of that coffee cake now. Would you care to join me?"

"That'd be nice," I said.

She cut us both a slice of cake and made us a fresh pot of coffee. As the coffee brewed, she said, "I can't imagine anything more heartbreaking than losing a child, and I want to help Lorinda any way I can. That's why I agreed to let her hold her séance here." She poured the coffee into cups, brought them over to the table where she'd already placed the slices of cake, and sat down opposite me. "But I can't do anything to jeopardize my space at Shops on Main. I've enjoyed greater success in that location than anywhere else I've ever been."

"Maybe Lorinda can talk with Mrs. Meacham and make her understand that this is something she needs to do for her own peace of mind."

"I guess it's worth a shot."

"Does Mrs. Meacham have children?" I asked.

Connie nodded. "She has a son and a daughter...so you'd think she'd understand Lorinda's desperation."

"Who had my space before I rented it?"

She frowned. "A man who owned a wine shop. He wasn't there for very long, though. And he didn't make an effort to get to know any of us."

"Huh…that surprises me. I guessed that whoever Mark was dating owned the shop."

"Oh, uh….no."

"Then who was he dating? Or was he dating anyone at Shops on Main? Was he lying to his mother about his love life to keep her off his back?"

"No," Connie said. "Mark was seeing Janice."

"Janice? From upstairs? The jewelry lady?"

She nodded.

"Really? But…she's…you know…she's old enough to be his mother."

"I know. Janice generally prefers dating younger men. She says they make her feel youthful."

"Is that why Janice didn't come to the séance today? Was reaching out to Mark just too painful for her?"

"It's more that Janice didn't want Lorinda to know about her. I doubt it was anything serious—Janice's flings never are. But Mark had kept the relationship secret from his mother, telling Janice that Lorinda wouldn't understand."

I thought that was probably an understatement, but I didn't voice my opinion.

"Given the fact that all three of them lived in the same town, I imagine it was difficult to be discreet," Connie continued, "but somehow they managed. Janice confided to me that all the sneaking around was fun."

I sipped my coffee. "What was Mark like?"

"At first, he came across as a real go-getter, but I think that was mostly for show. I expressed my concerns to him one day about not putting too many eggs in one basket. I mean, how much call can there be for people who only design websites these days when there are numerable options to easily design your own?" She shrugged. "But he balked at the idea of diversifying into marketing or advertising. He said he liked to program and that was it. He could be a bit...full of himself."

"I suppose his unwillingness to branch out was why his business was going under, and he was unable to pay his rent."

"I guess it was," Connie said. "I know from experience that small business owners have to work extremely hard or else they fail."

My bite of coffee cake stuck in my throat as I wondered if I had what it took to be a successful business owner.

Chapter Six

After leaving Connie's house, I went to visit Grandpa Dave. When I pulled into the driveway, I could see that the door to his workshop was open. I parked, got out, and strode toward the workshop.

Grandpa's workshop was ultra-neat. It was more organized than any room in my house. Shelves and cabinets lined three walls, and a pegboard held all of his hand tools. He had two mobile tool carts and a wet/dry vacuum in one corner. A table saw occupied a large portion of the center of the room, and a miter saw station was set up against the back wall. A scroll saw, a circular saw, and a jigsaw were usually kept in a cabinet near the miter saw station. Today, Grandpa was using the scroll saw at his workbench on the left side of the shop.

"Hi!" I called when he'd stopped the ratcheting of the saw for a moment.

"Hi, Pup! Be with you in just a minute!"

I stepped closer to see what he was carving out and was pleased to see that it was an elegant capital letter A.

"Can't let a body surprise you, can you, Pup?"

Gayle Leeson

"I'm sorry," I said, but I was sure he could tell I wasn't.

He backed away from the saw at last and held up the *A*.

"It's beautiful. I love it."

"Yeah, well, it's going on your shelf." He nodded toward the right of the shop where a beautiful walnut shelf sat.

With a quick intake of breath, I hurried over to examine it. The bottom shelves were wide and deep to accommodate bolts of fabric. The top shelves were tall and narrow for my books. Between the two top shelves was a cabinet with double doors.

Grandpa Dave had come up behind me, and I turned and gave him a bear hug.

He chuckled. "I'm glad you like it. But it's not finished yet. I still need to get the scrollwork—and this *A*—across the top. It'll be done by tonight, though, and I can bring it to your shop tomorrow morning."

"I had you a key made." I reached into my pocket and pulled out the shop key. "I figure it's always good to have an extra, and I'd rather you have it than put it somewhere at home and forget where it is."

"Thank you, ma'am." He took the key and placed a smudge of the varnish he was using for my shelf on it. "When that dries, I'll put it on my keyring."

I smiled. Grandpa Dave had always taught me to differentiate my keys in some way so I'd know which one was which. I used nail polish.

"So, how'd the séance go?" he asked.

"Not very well. Mark didn't show up." I frowned. "When his mother arrived, she thought I'd been dating Mark. I told her no, that I'd only met him once. And then after the séance, Connie told me it was Janice who Mark had been seeing."

"Janice…have I met her yet?"

"No. She's old enough to have been Mark's mother, though. I guess that's why Mark was keeping her identity a secret from his mom."

"You think this Janice might've killed Mark in a lovers' quarrel?"

"I doubt it," I said. "Janice doesn't strike me as the type of person who'd want to get her well-manicured hands dirty."

"Could the murderer be someone from her past then— an ex, maybe, who was jealous of Mark? Or it could've been someone Mark had been involved with. You always have to consider the lovers—or so they say on the crime shows."

"Anything's possible, I guess. I'm confident the police will figure it all out soon." I kissed his cheek. "Thanks for all your hard work. You've been such a tremendous help."

"Are you off then?"

I nodded. "I need to run home and then I'm going back by the shop...you know, to see how things are going there."

"I know. You're going to talk with Max." He grinned. "Tell her I said hi."

When I stopped at the house, I was pleased to see that my shop door sign had been delivered. I tore into the box to see how it looked and was delighted both that it had turned out just as I'd expected and that I'd paid to have it delivered by express mail. I was eager to get the sign onto my door, so I took it, Jazzy in her carrier, and the materials for the dress I'd been working on to the shop.

Connie's door was open, but she was busy with a customer when I entered the building. I went on into my shop, closed the door, and let Jazzy out of her carrier. The cat immediately ran to the writing desk where Max sat reading.

"Oh, hello." Max looked up at me and smiled. "You two are just in time. I've finished my book."

Jazzy hopped up onto the desk and stared at Max.

"I like you too," she said. "You're very pretty. What's your name?"

"Jasmine," I supplied. "But I call her Jazzy."

"Jazzy. That suits her." Max left the desk and followed me into the atelier. "That crazy old lady in the book I read solved the murder. The police didn't even have a clue until she told them who did it. Are you thinking what I'm thinking?"

"I seriously doubt it."

Jazzy had followed us and was now staring up at Max.

"She likes me. I'd love to be able to pick her up and give her a cuddle."

"That's what you were thinking?" I asked.

"No. I was thinking that you and I are every bit as clever as that old lady in the book and that we should solve Mark's murder."

"The big difference between you, me, and the old lady in the book is that fictional characters don't get killed for sticking their noses into other peoples' business."

"I must disagree with you there. Being killed because you were nosy is probably the most likely cause of fictional murder."

"Okay…which further shores up my argument that we need to leave the solving of Mark's murder to the police." Hoping to change the subject, I asked Max if she was aware that Mark had been involved with Janice.

"Yes, I knew about that. I don't believe it was anything serious, at least, not for Janice. She was always rushing off to the far corner of her office where she could stand and look out the window as she spoke with someone in hushed tones. I'm sure it was another man." She raised her brows. "You can always tell when a woman is talking with a man she's involved with—or wants to be involved with."

"What about Mark? Do you think he was seeing anyone else?"

"I'm not aware of any secret phone calls or anything of that nature as far as he was concerned."

"Did he have a lot of clients coming in?"

"As in pretty women or in general?" Max asked.

"In general. I know his business must have been failing because he was losing his lease."

"From what I could tell, Mark's business came in fits and starts. He also did a lot of work using his phone and his computer, so I don't know if foot traffic is an accurate judge of the amount of business he was doing."

"True."

"Still, Janice and Ford get a lot of foot traffic…and so do Connie and the Petermans. And none of them are losing their lease, so…"

"Connie and I were talking about Mark earlier today and saying that it was a shame his business was going under."

"What's a real shame is that he got murdered before he got the chance to turn things around."

I frowned. "What do you mean?"

"I heard him on the phone a day or two before he was killed telling someone that he was about to get an influx of cash."

"I wonder if maybe Mark was going to propose to Janice—if he thought of her as his meal ticket or something."

She shook her head. "While I'm not discounting your idea, I'm not sold on it. Is Janice really as well-to-do as she wants everyone to believe? I'm thinking no." She inclined her head. "Oh, it completely slipped my mind—how'd the séance go?"

"Not well. There was no sign of Mark."

"I'm not surprised. I think he's gone on. But, let's talk about something more exciting. What are you wearing for your photo shoot with Mr. Handsome tomorrow?"

"I'm planning to wear as many of my custom outfits as I have, including the two on the mannequins and one of the *prête-a-porter* dresses I'm making."

"The way he caught you yesterday was so romantic. Didn't you find him breathtakingly fabulous?"

My first instinct was to say yes, but I answered carefully. "Jason is gorgeous, but there's no point in thinking there's any romance brewing between the two of us. I mean, most likely, he's already taken."

{ 83 }

Gayle Leeson

"I didn't see a wedding ring on his finger. Don't be such a wet blanket. The man's the elephant's eyebrows—let's enjoy having him around."

There came a knock at the door that led from the atelier into the kitchen. I opened it to find Connie standing there looking bemused.

"I thought I heard you talking—" She broke off when she noticed Jazzy. "Oh! That's who you were talking to. Isn't she a pretty little thing? Hey, kitty. Hey, there."

I explained that her name was Jazzy, short for Jasmine.

"Lovely," said Connie. "What's she so enchanted with?"

I noticed that Jazzy was staring at Max.

"Who knows? Cats are nothing if not enigmatic."

"Isn't that the truth? I was just getting ready to make a pot of chamomile tea. Would you like some?"

"I'd love a cup. Thank you."

When Connie returned with two cups of tea, we sat on the navy chairs by the window.

"You've done a delightful job with the shop. It looks beautiful."

"Thanks," I said.

She nodded toward one of the mannequins. "Those dresses are stunning. Have you done any others?"

"I have." I took out my phone and showed her some of my completed projects as well as some of my sketched

{ 84 }

designs. "I fashioned myself a lookbook and put it on my website, but I need to add more to it."

"What's a lookbook?"

"It's a collection of my work." I smiled. "Most designers have a new lookbook every season, but I don't have enough designs to do that yet."

"You will have." Connie raised her teacup in salute.

I raised mine back and then took a sip. The tea really was good…and calming.

"Did you always want to be a fashion designer?" Connie asked.

"Kind of…" I gave her a sheepish grin. "I did always want to be, but my parents thoroughly discouraged it. They wanted me to have a paying job. So, I went to college and got a degree in business management with a minor in entrepreneurship."

"That worked out wonderfully then, didn't it? Now you have all the business tools—as well as the creative ability—to run your own business."

"How about you?" I asked. "Did you always want to have your own home goods shop?"

"No, not really. I was content being a stay-at-home mom until my children went to middle school and didn't need me as much anymore. Then I decided that if I didn't get out of the house, I'd go bonkers."

"And that led you to start your own business?"

"Not at first. At first, I tried to work for other people, but that did not go well. Whenever my children would call from school sick and need to come home, I'd leave. Whenever there was a snow day, I had to take a snow day too. That sort of thing does not go over well with most employers."

"I guess not."

She shrugged. "*C'est la vie*. I thought about it, decided to lease my own shop so I could come and go as I needed, and the rest is history. I've been here for five years."

"That's great. I'm glad you found such a successful niche."

"Me, too. I—"

A scream reverberated throughout the house.

Connie and I stared at each other for only a second before putting our teacups down on the round table and hurrying into the hallway.

Frank and Ella had come out of their shop too.

"It came from upstairs," Frank supplied, pointing up at the ceiling but showing no desire to investigate further.

Connie and I hurried up the steps to find Janice standing in the middle of the hallway, her face streaked with tears. Ford and Mrs. Meacham were trying to comfort her, but they weren't having much luck.

She kept saying over and over, "I can't believe it. I can't believe it. Why would someone break into my shop?"

Chapter Seven

As I got ready for my photo shoot with Jason the next morning, my mind drifted back to the mess the intruder had left of Janice's shop. Jewelry—much of it broken—had been flung onto the floor. None of it had been taken, so it appeared that throwing it onto the floor had been merely an act of spite. The police surmised the intruder was frustrated at not finding any cash in the ransacked desk. Janice said she didn't have a cash box and that she kept her money on her at all times.

Max hadn't seen anything because she'd been too absorbed in a new book—this one an Agatha Christie. However, she and I had discussed the possibility that it could have been Mark's killer who broke into Janice's office. After all, they had been involved with each other. It made sense that if Mark was murdered because of something he knew, his killer might feel the need to determine if Mark had confided the information to his lover.

"Did anyone point that fact out to the police?" Max had asked.

"No. I don't think Janice wants the detectives to know the two were dating."

Max tsked. "Makes you wonder what else she could be hiding, doesn't it?"

"It's none of my business."

She lifted and dropped one shoulder. "Well, if the police don't have all the information…"

I didn't take the bait, so Max continued.

"Someone who does have all the information needs to investigate."

"Let's hope someone either has or will tell the police about Janice's affair with Mark, and then they'll have all the information."

She wagged an index finger between her herself and me. "You and I are going to be the ones to figure this thing out." With a wink and a nod, she disappeared.

I rolled my eyes, realizing that it would be nearly impossible to get the last word in an argument with a ghost.

Now I looked in the mirror and assessed my makeup. It was heavier than what I usually wore, but I knew it had to be so I wouldn't appear washed out in the photos. I added the final touch—a rich, berry lipstick—and added some curl to my hair.

It's important I look my best for Jason—for the photos! I mean, for the photos! Of course, that's the important thing…but it wouldn't hurt if Jason thought I looked nice too. Better than nice...pretty...pretty enough to ask out on a date.

I scowled at myself in the mirror. *He undoubtedly has a girlfriend...and would probably not be interested in me even if he doesn't.*

I wore a jean skirt, white t-shirt, and red flats to the shop. I carried my other outfits in a dress bag, shoes in a rolling backpack, and jewelry and makeup (in case touch-ups were necessary) in a train case. I hung my bag on the clothes rack and placed the train case on the worktable. I took the green evening gown off the mannequin and stepped behind the Oriental screen to put it on.

"Amanda, it's Jason!" came a voice from the front room.

"Be there in just a second," I replied. "I hope it's okay if we start with the evening gown."

"Perfect. I'll get set up."

When I stepped into the front room wearing the emerald gown, gold strappy sandals, and dangling pearl earrings, Jason gave a low whistle.

"You look stunning."

I smiled, feeling my face flush at the compliment. "Thank you." I glanced around at all his light stands with umbrellas and boxes attached. "This is impressive."

He chuckled. "I try." He tilted his head and studied me for a moment.

Gayle Leeson

His scrutiny made me uncomfortable, and I looked around the room to see if Max was there. It would be just like her to pop up and get me even more flustered.

"Let's start you out there by the fireplace," Jason said.

I crossed the room, and he instructed me to stand with my back to him and look over my shoulder.

"We want to show off the back of that gown. And the back of that woman," he added with a grin.

I blushed again and hoped my cheeks wouldn't appear too pink in the photos. Of course, I supposed Jason could doctor that up. That was the great thing about photography these days—just about anything could be fixed.

He took several more shots in different positions by the fireplace and then asked me to move to the window. I posed sitting on one of the wingback chairs as well as standing by the window.

Finally, Jason announced that we shouldn't let that fabulous staircase go to waste. "Let's go out and take some photos there."

"But people will be coming in," I said.

"That's all right. They don't bother me."

They'll bother me...maybe even more than Max would. I didn't voice my opinion. I merely smiled and moved out into the hallway.

"Go up the steps—all the way to the first landing," Jason instructed. "Then turn and come back down."

I climbed the stairs, carefully ignoring Connie and her customer who'd come out to watch.

"Amanda!" Jason called.

I turned to look back at him.

"Perfect." He snapped the photo. "Now give me a smile." Snap. "Great. Proceed please."

"That gown is breathtaking," Connie's customer said. "My granddaughter is going to prom this year, and she'd look gorgeous in that."

"Have her drop in," Connie said. "Amanda just opened Designs on You, and I'm sure she'd love to make your granddaughter a dress like that."

I smiled, pleased that Connie was helping with PR. I'd have to remember to thank her later. I turned on the landing and could hear the camera clicking as Jason moved around near the bottom of the staircase taking shot after shot.

"Pause…that's good…now slowly walk toward me please."

"And that young man," Connie's customer said. "Wonder what he'd charge to do photographs?"

"He'll have an office upstairs starting on Monday, so I'm sure you could stop by," Connie said. "I imagine there will be high school seniors from all over the region hitting him up pretty soon, so I'd try to schedule with him early."

Janice came in through the back door, strode through the hall, and gazed around at the scene. "What's going on here?"

"Jason is photographing some of my designs," I said, as she neared the bottom of the staircase.

"Humph. Too bad so much of my jewelry got destroyed. I could've sold you some nice accessories."

I let that comment pass. Janice had been through a lot these past few days. Jason and I went back into Designs on You.

"I need to send Connie some chocolates or something," he said. "She was really talking us up out there."

"I heard and was thinking the same thing."

"Great minds…" He winked.

He was so handsome…those tropical ocean eyes…that full mouth…

Max snapped her fingers causing me to blink. "Snap out of it, darling. We don't want him to think you're desperate."

"So…what's next?" I asked.

"You tell me. I'm at your service."

Max sighed. "I see why you're looking all dopey now. You need to give it right back to him."

"I don't know how…"

At Jason's questioning look, I added, "—to choose. I don't know how to choose."

He nodded toward the dress form wearing the *prête a porter* dress. "What about that one?"

"All right. That one it is." I took the dress off the form and went behind the screen to change.

"I need help with these buttons," Max said.

"I need help with these buttons?" I echoed.

"Sure, no problem." Jason stepped around the screen and began unfastening the pearl buttons.

My eyes flew to Max, who was laughing and clapping her hands.

"How did you manage to get this on earlier?" Jason asked. "Was somebody here to help you?"

"No…and it wasn't easy," I said. "I can be quite the contortionist when I need to be."

Max gave me two thumbs up, and my eyes widened when I realized how that must have sounded.

"Good to know." Jason finished unbuttoning the gown. "Is there anything else I can do?"

"Oooh…loaded question," Max said. "So many good things you can say to that. How about 'not at the moment'?"

"Um…not at the moment."

"All right. I'm just in the other room if you need me."

"Thank you."

Max fanned her face with both hands. "That man was looking at the small of your back the way a child looks at a chocolate cake."

"Max!"

"What's that?" Jason called from the front room.

"I…I was just saying that…Max…Mara…has been an influence on some of my designs."

"Good save," said Max.

"Cool," said Jason.

I quickly changed into the ready-to-wear dress, changed the pearl earrings for jet buttons, and put on black and white pumps. I pulled my hair back in a clip and placed a wide-brimmed white hat with a black grosgrain ribbon onto my head.

"Fantastic!" Jason said, raising the camera to his eye. "Give me a three-sixty."

I did a full turn.

"Great." He lowered the camera. "Let's take this one outside. Some street scenes will be fun."

"Sounds good to me," I said. The farther I could get away from Max right now the better. Who knew what my ghostly gal pal would have me saying next?

When we returned to Shops on Main, Grandpa Dave was there with the finished shelf. Frank and Ford were helping him lug it inside the building. I rushed to unlock the door to Designs on You, while Jason hurried to help the men.

The shelf was a masterpiece. All the vendors came to look at it, and upon hearing the noise from out in the hall, Mrs. Meacham did too.

"Why, this is beautiful," Mrs. Meacham said, running her hand along the smooth walnut wood. "How long have you been doing carpentry work?"

"Nearly all my life," said Grandpa Dave. "It's just a hobby, but I enjoy it. Before I retired, it got me through the stresses of my day. Now it's merely a relaxing but productive way to pass the time."

"You call that passing the time?" Connie asked as she came into the room. "That scrollwork across the top is magnificent."

Grandpa beamed. "I appreciate it, but I just wanted to make Amanda something she could be proud of."

I kissed his cheek. "I am proud of it. I love it. It's wonderful."

"I don't want to hold you up," he began.

"Nonsense," I interrupted, introducing him to Jason. "We have one more outfit to do, and then I thought we could all go to lunch—well, anyone who wants to go, that is."

Connie, Frank, and Ford all said they needed to get back to work. Mrs. Meacham said she needed to get home—some of the grandchildren were coming by later. But Grandpa Dave and Jason said they'd love to go to lunch.

I changed into a sort of steampunk-inspired black and gold brocade jacket that was short in the front and calf-length in the back. I paired the jacket with black silk pants and strappy black heels and was grateful the air conditioning was working well in the shop.

Jason decided that the outfit inspired some moodier shots. Using only one light source, he shot images of me standing both in front of the Oriental screen and by the shelf Grandpa Dave had made. He then pulled one of the navy chairs away from the window and put it near the fireplace for some seated shots.

"These will be beautiful," he said, looking at the digital images on his camera's screen. "I believe you're going to be really happy with them."

"Thank you so much for doing this. Let me get changed, and I'll buy you guys lunch."

"You don't have to do that," Jason said.

I looked from him to Grandpa and back again. "It's my pleasure."

"It isn't every day you get to take two handsome men to lunch," Max said.

Starting slightly because I hadn't been aware Max was there, I echoed my friend's sentiment before going behind the screen to change.

Max clasped her hands together. "I can hardly wait to see the final photographs. They're all going to be wonderful."

"How can you be so sure?" I whispered. "I might look like a troll in all of them."

"Nonsense. You don't give yourself enough credit. You're quite lovely."

"Thanks."

"You'll look like a queen. And you can make an enlargement of the one you like best and put it over the fireplace."

"Wouldn't that seem a little much?"

"Amanda, you need help with anything?" Grandpa called.

"Nope. Fine. Be right there."

Max laughed. "No, it wouldn't be a little much. It would be great for business—yours and Jason's. And that is his excuse for doing this."

"Excuse?" I remembered to whisper this time.

"Oh, darling, he wants to get to know you. Embrace it."

I finished dressing and stepped back into the sitting area. Max threw Grandpa Dave a kiss, and he winked at her. I managed to avoid rolling my eyes at the two of them. Jason probably thought I was nutty already for "mumbling to myself" while changing clothes.

Once we'd placed our orders at the café, I broached the subject of the photographs.

"Jason, I do wish you'd let me pay you for your work this morning."

"Nothing doing. It was my idea, and I'm sure it will help promote my business."

"I'm afraid I don't have a client base yet. It might be a while before you get any work from your photographs being featured in Designs on You."

"I wouldn't say that," Grandpa said. "I brought my work into your shop first thing this morning, and Connie has already asked me to come by and quote her a price on redoing her kitchen cabinets. So, see? The potential for getting work through your shop is greater than you think."

"Besides, your client list will likely grow faster than you think it will. My friend Garic Stephens owns a fashion design business called Lavelle in Glade Spring. Garic is originally from Chicago, and I believe he had some reservations when he first opened, but his business is booming."

"That's fantastic," I said. "I'd love to talk with him sometime."

"I do a lot of work with him. I'll ask him to stop by the next time he's in Abingdon, and I'll bring him downstairs to your shop."

"Thank you."

"Have you always been a photographer?" Grandpa Dave asked Jason.

"Yes, sir, as a hobby anyway. I went to college and got a photography degree, and I worked in department store photo labs and freelanced until I could save enough to open my own business. My previous location wasn't that great, so I jumped at the chance to lease a space at Shops on Main."

"You had a better plan than I did," I said. "I saw the space and decided—overnight—that I wanted to open my own business."

Jason raised his glass of soda. "To your courage."

"Here, here." Grandpa Dave raised his glass as well.

I joined in the fun, and we clinked our glasses together. I just hoped my courage didn't turn out to be a case of foolhardy temerity.

I returned to Shops on Main after lunch. Grandpa and Jason got into their vehicles and went their separate ways. I told Grandpa I'd see him tomorrow at his house. Jazzy and I often went over on Sundays to spend the afternoon with him.

I didn't see Max, but I prepared my tablet to stream *The Thin Man*. I left a sticky note instructing Max to hit the play button to enjoy the movie.

Gathering up my things to leave, I heard a noise upstairs and realized that either Janice or Ford must be in the building. I took my garment bag and train case to my car and saw that a pickup truck was the only other vehicle in the parking lot. I couldn't in a million years imagine Janice driving a truck and guessed it must be Ford who was still there. I decided to go check out his shop and thank him again for his help.

I went back inside the building and up the stairs to Antiquated Editions. The door was closed, so I tapped lightly. When he didn't answer right away, I thought I must be mistaken about Ford's still being there; but then he called for me to come in.

I walked inside and smiled at the beefy man standing behind the counter. "I just wanted to thank you again for helping Grandpa Dave with the furniture both yesterday and today."

"No problem. It was my pleasure."

"If there's ever anything I can do for you, please let me know."

He chuckled. "If I ever need a pretty dress, I'll know who to come to."

I smiled. "Well, I don't make men's clothing, but I can hem pants or tailor a shirt if you ever need it."

"Good to know."

"Mind if I look around a bit?"

"Help yourself."

As I wandered around the shop, I continued to talk with Ford. "Is it weird working here now...you know, after what happened to Mark?"

"A little."

"I can tell Grandpa is worried about my being here. He told me to never work too late and find myself here alone."

"Aw, honey, I don't think you've got anything to fear here. I mean, it's always a good idea to be aware of your surroundings and not to work too late by yourself no matter where you are, but I don't think Mark's death was a random killing."

"You don't?"

He shook his shaggy head. "I believe Mark had a lot of personal problems and that one of those came back to bite him."

"Really? You think Mark was involved in something shady?"

Ford raised his hands. "I'm not one to speak out of turn or poorly of the dead—and Mark seemed like a nice enough kid, given the little I knew about him—but the boy's money had to be going somewhere, and it wasn't being put toward his rent or growing his business."

"Maybe he just wasn't making that much. I mean, is web design still a lucrative business for an entrepreneur when it's so easy for people to make websites on their own?"

"I couldn't say. You would think a designer would do better working for a corporation or something, wouldn't you?"

I stopped at a locked case where there was an obviously old copy of *A Tale of Two Cities*. I caught my breath as I turned back toward Ford. "Is this a first edition?"

"Yes, ma'am." He beamed. "One of my pride and joy books. It's been professionally re-backed, but as much of the original back strip as possible was left in place."

"It must be worth a fortune."

"To me, it's priceless. In that same case there, I have a first edition of *The Old Man and The Sea*, a first edition Edgar Allan Poe *Tales of Mystery and Imagination* illustrated by Arthur Rackham, and a first edition of Louisa May Alcott's *Little Men*."

"That's fantastic!"

"Thank you. That's my treasure chest." He got a dreamy look in his dark eyes. "Did you know that a first edition of Poe's first book *Tamerlane and Other Poems* was sold at auction in 2009 for $662,500? It set a new record for a work of American literature."

"Tamerlane...I've never even heard of it."

"You'll have to look it up. It's said that Poe wrote the work before he was fourteen years old and it was published when he was eighteen."

"Do you have a copy of it here?"

"No. I'm sure you can find a cheap copy of it in paperback online, if you're interested. The original book was so rare that a Christie's auction house expert called it the 'black tulip of U.S. literature.' Only fifty copies were printed in 1857."

"Weren't you worried about your 'treasure chest' when Janice's shop was robbed?" I asked.

"At first, I was a bit concerned, but the fact that nothing valuable was taken from Janice's shop made me feel that we didn't have a thief running around."

"Do you think the break-in was connected to Mark's murder? They were dating, you know."

Ford guffawed. "Who are you? Nancy Drew?"

"Just a concerned new shop owner," I said, feeling a blush creeping up my face.

"Well, you might be right that whoever broke into Janice's shop was looking for something other than jewelry or money. But either way, don't worry so much. Everything is going to be fine. I've been here for four years, and I've never had the first hint of a problem."

"Thanks." After buying a beautiful leather-bound copy of *A Tale of Two Cities*—nothing rare, just one of my favorite books—I told Ford again how much I appreciated his help with the furniture, wished him a good weekend, and left.

I hoped he was right and that the nightmare of Mark's death was behind us. But I had a feeling that it wasn't.

Chapter Eight

I went home and worked on a ready-to-wear dress for the rest of the afternoon. I wanted to be able to showcase a range of sizes I was able to work with, rather than have my customers come in, see the one size—mine—on display and believe that was all I could or would do. I was proud of the fact that I could design a piece to flatter each woman, no matter what her size or shape.

I took a dinner break at about six o'clock. I went into the kitchen, opened my laptop, and did a search for quick and easy recipes. While cooking wasn't my passion, I did enjoy it, and I liked trying new dishes. I found a tuna casserole that baked in a pie crust. Fortunately, I already had a frozen pie crust, and I always kept tuna on hand. The recipe called for shredded cheese, which I didn't have, but I did have some single serving sizes of Colby jack in the fridge that I could cut up. I quickly prepared the casserole and placed it in the preheated oven.

While the casserole baked, I decided to see if I could find any information on my great-grandfather—the one Max had dated. I recalled that his name was George

Channing. I searched for George Channing and 1929. Nothing. But, of course, my great-grandpa wouldn't be found through a random search engine inquiry—he wasn't a celebrity or anything. I went back to the Abingdon Virginian archives, and there I hit pay dirt.

There was a photo of George—nice looking, I could see a resemblance to Grandpa Dave—returning from a tour of duty in Nicaragua. He'd been a marine, and he looked dapper and brave in his uniform. No wonder Max had taken such a shine to him. I saved the photo to my phone.

I continued looking through the search results for George Channing and saw that in December of 1930, George had attended a party with Dorothy Englebright. Surely, this woman was Max's sister. But why would George be with her? I had the brief, perverse thought: You don't think Dorothy pushed Max down the stairs so she could have George, do you?

I immediately felt guilty for having such a thought. But it wouldn't quit nagging at me either.

After dinner, I finished the dress before taking my new book and going to bed. I put on my pajamas and propped my pillows against the headboard. Before leaning back, I gently ran my fingers across the embossed title—*A Tale of Two Cities*. My mind drifted back to being in Ford's shop. I imagined much of Ford's business would be conducted online. How many people were walking in off the street and plunking down hundreds—or even thousands—of dollars for some of the rarest editions? Of course, until today, I'd never considered I'd be walking into Antiquated Editions and paying sixty dollars for this leather-bound copy of *A Tale of Two Cities*. But the book was one of my favorites…and it was more of a way to pay Ford back for his help than anything…although I did love the book. I hugged it to my chest. Maybe Ford got more foot traffic than I had initially imagined.

Janice was another person whose business was hard for me to fathom. From what I could tell, Janice had some nice pieces of jewelry, but I'd never seen her actually making any jewelry. So, were the pieces handmade by Janice? Or by someone else?

To the best of my ability, I put Shops on Main out of my mind as I sank into the pillows and opened my book.

It was the best of times, it was the worst of times, it was the age of wisdom, it was the age of foolishness, it was the epoch of belief, it was the epoch of incredulity, it was the season of Light, it was the season of Darkness…

I drifted off to sleep and dreamed that I was Lucie Manette, Jason was Sydney Carton. And Janice was Madame DeFarge.

After getting up, feeding the cat, and taking a leisurely bath, I put Jazzy in her carrier and went to Grandpa Dave's house. When I arrived, the first thing I did—after letting Jazzy out of the carrier—was to show Grandpa the photographs of his grandfather.

He smiled and got a faraway look in his eyes as he gazed the photo of George in his dress uniform. "I remember this picture. Nanny had it on her bedroom wall."

"He was handsome. I can see a resemblance between the two of you."

"My parents died before you were born, but my mother looked like Papaw. She was a striking woman."

"I'm sure she was. I wish I could've known her."

"Me too, Pup."

I swiped the photo away to reveal the next one, the picture of George with Dorothy Englebright at the society party. "Is that your grandmother?"

He shook his head. "I don't know who that is." He squinted at the caption. "Dorothy Englebright... Max's sister?"

"That's what I'm thinking. You don't think she'd have shoved Max down the stairs out of jealousy...do you?" I kept my voice light, but I couldn't help but think there could be something more to Max's fall than even Max imagined.

"I believe Mark's death has you imagining murderers around every corner. Are you sure you're going to be all right working in that place?"

I assured him that I was. "So...what are you thinking for lunch today?"

"How about chicken pot pie? It'll take a while to make, but it'll be worth it."

"Deal. And while it bakes, we can watch something on TV." I told him about leaving the tablet ready to show Max *The Thin Man*. "I hope she was able to watch it."

"If she can use the tablet to read books, she should be able to watch the movie," he said as we strolled into the kitchen.

Grandpa Dave got a round casserole dish out of the cabinet and preheated the oven. "If you'll start cleaning and chopping some carrots, I'll get started on the crust."

As we worked, our conversation turned back to Shops on Main.

"It's great that you're giving Connie a quote on her kitchen cabinets," I said. "Although, when I was there, it didn't look as if anything in her house needed refurbishing."

"Has a nice one, does she?"

"She does." I took the carrots to the sink and picked up a vegetable brush. "Maybe she just wants something different."

"That's a possibility. People get tired of looking at the same old things day after day." He winked. "That's why I try to avoid mirrors."

"Oh, you don't. You look great and you know it. I don't believe Max would refer to you as a silver fox otherwise."

Grandpa colored slightly as he chuckled. "Where did she say she picked that phrase up?"

"From Janice. She owns the jewelry shop upstairs."

"Right. The man-eater."

"She is...um...kinda bumptious...isn't she?"

"Bumptious?" He raised his brows and shook his head. "If you're trying to find a nice way to say the woman is brazen, annoying, and in-your-face...then, sure, she's kinda bumptious."

"I just feel bad for her. She was dating Mark—"

"—who was young enough to be her son..."

"And then her shop got ransacked," I continued. "It just seems like she's going through a rough time."

"Be careful, Pup. Keep in mind that you don't know any of these people. If someone broke into Janice's shop to find something—and it doesn't appear that anything was taken—then whatever that person was looking for could've been what got Mark killed."

I frowned. "What do you mean?"

"Think about it. Mark might've been killed because he knew something that Janice was hiding. All I'm saying is to be careful with everybody at Shops on Main...at least, until you know them better—a lot better."

After eating lunch, tidying the kitchen, and watching a show about carpentry—Grandpa loved it, and I found it interesting too—we decided to go to Designs on You to make sure everything was shipshape for the next day.

I was glad that Grandpa didn't say much as he drove. I'd been afraid he might ask me if I was excited about my grand opening or if I'd told my parents about my shop yet. I hadn't told them. I wanted the shop to be successful first, or at least, modestly successful. Since I only talked with my parents about once a month, I justified my actions by telling myself that I wasn't misleading them but merely waiting to surprise them.

Despite the fact—or maybe because of the fact—that we hadn't discussed my opening the shop to the public tomorrow, my heart was pounding as I unlocked the main door at Shops on Main and then my shop door.

"What do we need to do?" Grandpa asked.

"There's not a lot to do," I said. "I don't have much to work with yet."

He nodded toward the bolts of fabric I had stacked on my work table. "How about we put those on the shelf?"

"Yes, that'd be great." I took a bolt of red fabric and stood it up on one of the bottom shelves. I wondered where Max was...if she'd been able to watch her movie...if she'd liked it if she had seen it. Anything to get my mind off the worry that I finally gave voice to. "What if nobody comes tomorrow?"

"Of course, people will come!" He put the bolt of fabric he was holding onto the shelf before coming over and hugging me. "You've put out flyers, you and Jason attracted attention on the street yesterday, Connie is helping to spread the word..."

"But that's no guarantee people will come into the shop."

"If they don't, we'll throw a party!"

Grandpa started at the sound of Max's voice. "Don't do that. You'll give an old man a heart attack."

"If I weren't a spirit, I'd take that as a personal challenge." She grinned. "But back to this no customers thing. Of course, you'll have them, but if or when you want more, we'll simply have a party."

"Max has a point. A grand opening soiree a few weeks from now will be a wonderful way to welcome customers and to let them know what you're all about."

"By that time, Jason will have your photographs finished, and you can have them framed or put on canvases or whatever and displayed on your walls." Max twirled around, as if she were already imagining where the photos should be placed. "You'll serve canapes and wine, and people will be drawn to you like flies to manure."

I laughed. "Well, that's a flattering image."

"It will be the berries! Wait and see."

"I agree," said Grandpa. "And, Amanda, you can leave the party-planning to Max and me."

I stilled. "I hear someone upstairs."

"Yes, that's Jason," said Max. "I was upstairs looking over his shoulder at your photos before you arrived. They're marvelous."

"Really?"

Max nodded and then tilted her head as they heard footsteps on the stairs. "Dave, darling, why don't you and I go out onto the porch? I believe Jason is coming down to talk with Amanda."

He grinned. "Good idea."

I followed them out into the hallway.

Grandpa looked up and saw Jason on the stairs. "Hi, Jason. I'm going to go out and get some fresh air while Amanda puts the finishing touches on the shop for tomorrow's thundering hoard of customers."

"Thundering hoard? In my dreams," I said.

Jason came on down the steps and walked with me back into my shop. "I think the place looks great."

"Thank you."

"And I believe you might be surprised at how many people you'll find checking out your shop tomorrow. I won't say they'll all be customers, at least, not at first, but there will be a lot of people come in."

"How about you? Do you have any appointments set up for tomorrow?"

"I do," he said. "That's my advantage. I had a client list before I leased this space."

"I would like to see your studio."

He extended a hand toward the door. "After you."

As we walked up the staircase, I confessed that hearing his feet upstairs made me nervous. "I immediately thought of Mark, his killer, Janice's shop being ransacked. It's amazing how many things can flood your mind at once."

"It is. Hearing you guys down here gave me pause too. I thought I'd better come down and check it out."

"I'm glad you did. I mean, I wouldn't have bolted from the building or anything, but it's nice to know it was you."

"Hey, if you ever get scared while working here, always go to a safe place," said Jason. "Never talk yourself out of following your fear instinct."

He ushered me into his studio. The first thing I saw was a projection screen, which took up most of the far wall, and was surrounded by various lighting sources. A tall wooden stool stood in front of the screen. There were shelves that contained cameras and lenses and other photography stuff that I didn't recognize. Smaller screens, chairs, and other props were located throughout the room as well. A desk sat beneath the window, the chair currently facing away from it and the blinds drawn.

"This is really nice," I said. "Will you do most of your shoots here?"

"Some. I also do location shots. I go to schools and local parks and landmarks for senior portraits. I do weddings. I shot you in your shop and on the street because I knew those would be the most flattering." He nodded toward the laptop on his desk. "I haven't finished touching up the photos yet, but would you like to see what I've got?"

"I would."

Jason pulled one of the prop chairs over to the desk for me before he sat on the desk chair and opened the laptop.

Gayle Leeson

The screen filled with an image of me in the emerald evening gown looking over my shoulder.

"That's one of my favorites," Jason said. "But I'm not bragging—not on myself, anyway—when I tell you they're all good." He clicked a button, and the screen changed to a slideshow.

We both smiled as we watched the screen, and I wondered if he was remembering the shoot as fondly as I was.

When we got to the end, Jason explained that after he'd touched up all the photos, he'd give them to me on a disk, and I could make whatever I wanted from them.

"If I were you, I'd make this one—" He was back to the original photo of me in the green gown. "—into a 24" x 36" canvas print and place it over your mantle."

"Will you help me determine what size prints I should get and where I should put them?"

"I'd be happy to." He looked back at the screen. "It's cool that you're so tight with your grandpa."

"Yeah. My parents live in Florida, and he's really great."

"Does he live with you?"

"No. I live in my parents' house, and he has a house in the country…about ten or fifteen minutes from here."

"Cool."

"So…who do you live with, Jason?" I immediately regretted saying the words and kept my eyes glued to the computer screen.

"A little white mutt named Rascal." He closed the laptop. "Will you be going out to celebrate tomorrow night?"

"I guess that depends on how the first day goes. Will you?"

"Maybe. Like you, I guess it depends."

"I should get back downstairs," I said.

"And I need to get home and feed Rascal. He's a bottomless pit."

"Thank you again for the photos. You do wonderful work."

"You're welcome, and you made it easy."

When I got back downstairs, Grandpa and Max were looking at the tablet.

"We're deciding what I should watch next," Max said. "I loved the movie you left for me."

"I'm glad you could watch it."

"So…did Jason show you photos?" she asked.

"He did. They're pretty good."

She scoffed. "Pretty good? They're fantastic! Wait until you see them, Dave. You'll love them."

"Jason is going to help me decide what size prints to get and where to put them. He thinks I should put one of me in the green evening gown over the mantle."

"I agree," said Max. "Has he asked you out on a proper date yet?"

"No." I lowered her voice. "He's probably dating someone."

"I don't think so. No photo on his desk—and he's a photographer, for goodness' sake. If he had a girlfriend, he'd have photos of her in his studio."

"Max has a point At least, don't knock yourself out of the running when you don't even know whether or not you have competition."

I was beginning to squirm under the spotlight. "Oh, Max, I have some photos to show you." I got out my phone and pulled up the picture of dashing George Channing in his uniform. "He was handsome."

"He certainly was." Max's face and her voice fell. She reached out her hand, although she knew she couldn't touch the image.

When Max's hand neared the phone, the image was replaced by the one of George with Max's sister Dorothy.

"Dot…" A sad, wistful smile briefly kissed her lips. "That was at the Christmas cotillion the year I died."

"Did George date Dorothy after…well…after?" I asked.

"No. They were only friends. They leaned on each other rather heavily after my death."

"That's good." I cleared my throat. "I was afraid Dorothy had pushed you down the stairs." My attempt at a laugh was feeble.

"Nonsense. Dot and I were inseparable."

"I'm afraid Amanda has let Mark's death influence everything she sees lately," Grandpa said.

"Yes, well, it was a shock to everyone...except the killer, I imagine." Max stared out into the hallway as if she was reliving her moment of death. "You know, I did feel a bit off the night I tumbled down the stairs. I wonder if I was sick or something."

Chapter Nine

After tossing, turning, and checking the clock throughout the night, I took extra care with my makeup Monday morning. I didn't want to look like a sleep-deprived zombie on the first morning Designs on You was open. Of course, worrying about opening day was what had made me look like a sleep-deprived zombie, but that was beside the point.

Once I'd concealed, contoured, accented, and highlighted my face, I put on a 1950s-inspired fuchsia sheath dress with a lattice neckline and nude wedge sandals.

I fed Jazzy and apologized to the cat for leaving her alone today. I had every intention of taking Jazzy with me tomorrow, but I needed to make sure I could keep the cat inside and away from that busy Main Street traffic while customers were coming in and out of the shop.

I arrived at Designs on You nearly an hour before I was scheduled to open. I was relieved to see Max standing in the middle of the waiting room in anticipation of my arrival.

Max gave a wolf whistle. "You look beautiful! Everything today is going to be the berries. Just you wait and see. You're talented, you know your onions, you're charming—why, you're simply the elephant's eyebrows!"

I laughed. "You always know just what to say."

"Thank you. I've had many, many years to come up with dialogue and delivery." Max nodded at my wringing hands. "Stop being a Nervous Nellie and enjoy today."

"I'm trying—I really am."

Connie entered after lightly tapping on the door. "I heard you giving yourself a pep talk. Maybe this will help." She held out a mug.

I took the mug and lifted it to her nose. "Cinnamon tea?"

"Kava tea, actually. It's supposed to relax you."

"Thank you. Let's sit." I took the mug and sat on one of the navy chairs by the window. "I'm so nervous."

"I figured you would be. That's why I came in early." She nodded toward the mug. "Drink up. I promise it'll help."

I sipped the tea and found that it was quite good. It had a cinnamon-y, chai-like flavor.

"I was anxious my first day too," said Connie. "But everything will be fine. You'll find that sometimes your business flows and sometimes it ebbs—just use both periods of time wisely. Use the flows to flourish and the ebbs to learn."

"Wise words," Max murmured.

I nodded.

Connie had left the door open, and Mrs. Meacham joined us.

"I see Connie is taking care of you," the older woman said with approval. "She's our caretaker, always brewing up potions to help us feel better."

"I made Amanda some Kava tea," Connie said with a smile.

"Ah, that's good. Soothes the nerves." Mrs. Meacham bobbed her head. "I'll be off then. But if you need anything, I'm right upstairs."

"Thank you," I said.

The words were barely out of my mouth before Ella hurried in.

"Hi, sweetie. I wanted to come over before the shop opens to wish you luck and to give you a ten-percent off coupon on a total purchase from Everything Paper."

"That's so generous," I said. "Thank you. I, too, will certainly extend a discount to my Shops on Main family. Anytime any of you want to buy anything, you'll get the friends and family discount—say, twenty-percent off?"

"Thank you, Amanda," said Connie. "I'll likely take you up on that sometime soon. I love clothes."

"Yes, well...my coupon is only good for one visit," Ella said. "So...you know, make it count. The more you buy, the bigger the discount! See you later." With that, she hurried off, presumably back to her shop.

Max gave a squeak of indignation as Connie shook with quiet laughter.

Connie gave my shoulder a warm squeeze. "I need to get to my post too, but I'll be back to check on you later. Would you like the door left open or closed?"

"Open, please...although I might make a sign tomorrow to keep it closed because I'm planning on bringing my cat to keep me company. Do you think that'll be okay?"

"I think it'll be great."

As soon as Connie left, Max asked, "Would you like for me to man the shop while you go buy one of everything they've got over there at Ella's place?"

"Tempting as that offer is, I'd better stick around since none of my customers would be able to see you."

"Suit yourself, darling, but that's a one-time-use coupon and it might be a limited-time offer as well. You can't be too careful."

"I'll take my chances," I said with a laugh.

My first customers were a pair of middle-aged to older women. One was tall, stout, and boisterous, and the other was mousy and less talkative. Both women wore capris, t-shirts, and sandals. They looked around for a moment before the tall one said, "Is this all you've got?"

"Yes...for now." I went on to explain the concept of the shop. "I'll have some ready-to-wear pieces, but most of my items will be custom made to the client's specifications."

"Hmph." The tall one stalked back out of the shop with her mousy friend in her wake.

The friend hurried back in moments later. Without the other woman and her overpowering personality, I could see that this woman wasn't mousy but merely delicate and soft-spoken.

"I accidentally-on-purpose left my handbag here," she said with a grin. "My granddaughter is getting married soon, and I'd love to come back in and talk with you when I have more time."

"Of course!" I strode over to the desk and retrieved a couple of business cards for the woman. "Come back anytime."

"Thank you. I find the notion of a custom dress simply marvelous. My granddaughter's fiance's aunt is kinda snobby, and I'd love to have a one-of-a-kind gown that would knock everybody's socks off...especially hers."

"I can certainly fix you right up. And if you'll tell me who the aunt is—" I said, with a conspiratorial wink, "—I'll make sure she doesn't outshine you."

"Oh, you just met her. She was the mouthy one."

Max threw back her head and laughed. As soon as the woman had scurried out with her purse, I gave into a fit of giggles myself.

Grandpa Dave brought an entire Dutch oven filled with chicken and dumplings at around eleven-thirty that morning. He came through the door, spoke with Max and me—who were the only ones in the shop at the time—and asked if he could warm his dish up in the kitchen.

"Sure. That looks wonderful, Grandpa. You know I love your chicken and dumplings."

"I wish I could taste them," Max said, peering into the pot. "They look delicious." She sighed. "A man as handsome as you who cooks? Ah, Dave, you make me wish I were alive."

Grandpa took the dish into the kitchen, removed the clear lid, and put it on a burner to warm. "I'll check around and see if anyone else wants some."

"Actually, I'd like to ask…if you don't mind watching the shop," I said. "I haven't been out of the shop all day, and I'll like to walk around a bit."

"She wants to go up and check on lover boy," said Max. "But that suits me. Stay here and talk with me, Silver Fox."

"Okay, scoot, Pup. The chicken and dumplings should be warm by the time you get back."

I started with Connie. She was with a customer, so I waited until the woman had paid for her purchase and had left the shop before asking Connie if she'd like to join us for chicken and dumplings for lunch.

"My grandpa made them. He's a wonderful cook, and…well, he spoils me. He brought enough for everyone."

"How thoughtful! I'd love some. Thank you!"

Next stop Everything Paper.

"Does your grandfather put celery in his chicken and dumplings?" Ella asked.

"No, ma'am. We don't particularly like the taste of celery in ours."

"Well, I put lots of celery in mine. We love it. Don't we, Frank?"

"Yeah, sure. I'll take you up on that offer, Amanda. Is Dave here now?"

"Yes, he's in Designs on You."

Gayle Leeson

"Good. See you in a few, Ella." With that, he was gone. So much for Max and Grandpa Dave having much of a conversation.

I headed upstairs. Mrs. Meacham thanked me for the offer but declined, saying she always goes home to make lunch for Mr. Meacham now that her husband is retired. Janice said she was watching her figure. Ford said he was meeting a friend for lunch but that it was good to know someone with a tried-and-true chicken and dumplings recipe. He said he hadn't had really good chicken and dumplings since his grandmother died.

I saved Jason for last. He said he would be delighted to have lunch with Grandpa and me.

As we walked downstairs toward the kitchen, Jason asked me how business was going.

"My first couple of customers were characters. One of them acted as if she were insulted by the very idea of my shop, but her friend came back in and said she'd like a one-of-a-kind dress for her granddaughter's wedding. She also let me in on the fact that she wanted to outshine her...well, I guess it would be her frenemy...who is the granddaughter's fiance's aunt."

"That sounds fantastic. Do you think they've booked a photographer yet?"

"I don't know. But when she comes back in, I'll definitely tell her she should come upstairs and talk with you."

"Thanks. Anybody else interesting come along?"

"I've had a few people stop in, and I sold one of the ready-to-wear dresses, so I'm happy at how the day is going."

"I'm glad. May I take you to dinner this evening to celebrate?"

"Yes, I'd like that."

Later that afternoon, I was working on a sketch for a new dress in the workroom while Max read at the desk in the reception area. The design was an evening gown inspired by a 1946 Butterick evening dress pattern. I was modifying the sweetheart neckline to be off the shoulders and to have rosettes go completely around the top. The dress had a fitted bodice and then fell gracefully to the floor.

I had a small rolling cart sitting next to me at the work table. The cart contained my pencils, erasers, pencil sharpeners, fine felt-tip black pens, watercolors, colored pencils, and markers. I mixed a bit of violet and white paint to get a mauve color and began painting the gown.

Gayle Leeson

Max drifted into the workroom and looked at the sketch. "That's really pretty."

"Thanks. I got to thinking that I've been designing mostly for myself, but now that I've opened Designs on You, I need to upgrade my lookbook to include things like bridesmaid and prom dresses."

The click-click-click of Janice's heels on the floor above caused both of us to look ceilingward.

"Third. Time. Today," I said. "Not that I'm counting."

"Once was too many." Max blew out a breath. "Why doesn't she stay in her shop where she belongs?"

"It sure doesn't seem as if Janice is as heartbroken about Mark as she was before Jason arrived." I immediately chastised myself. "I'm sorry. Maybe she's just trying to make Jason feel welcome."

Max snorted. "Yeah, and maybe I'm just a figment of your imagination."

A voice sounded from the other room. "Hello?"

"Hi!" I called. "Be right there."

When she entered the reception area, I recognized the woman I'd seen with Connie during the photo shoot on Saturday. The girl with her was undoubtedly her granddaughter.

"Welcome to Designs on You," I said. "It's great to see you again."

"I didn't know whether you'd remember me or not," the woman said. "You were so busy with your photos and everything...but I'm flattered that you did remember."

"Of course. You wanted to look at the green evening gown, right?"

"Yes, please. By the way, I'm Olga, and this is my granddaughter Taylor."

"Nice to meet you both." I took the gown off the mannequin and handed it to Taylor. "You can change right in there behind the Oriental screen."

Taylor smiled at her grandmother before hurrying off with the dress.

"If you need any help, let us know." I called.

"I'd better go with her and help her with those buttons," said Olga.

When the pair returned to the reception area, I ushered them back to the three-way mirror.

Taylor gasped. "I love it!"

"It looks really beautiful on you."

Taylor looked at Olga. "Can we get it, Grandma?"

"Let's talk with your mom first and make sure it's okay," Olga said, snapping some pictures of Taylor with her phone. "If she says it is, then yes, we'll come back and get it." She looked at me. "Do we need to put a deposit down on it?"

"Actually, if you buy the dress, you won't be getting this dress, but one custom made to fit Taylor. She can even get the dress in a different color, if she'd like."

"What? I can have a prom dress made specifically for me?" Taylor asked. "Nobody else will have one like it?"

"That's right."

"That's so lit!" Taylor hugged Olga.

"That *is* lit," Olga said. "Go ahead and get changed. I made some photos for your mom." As Taylor went behind the Oriental screen, Olga told me that lit was a good thing. "Oh, you probably already knew that."

"I didn't," Max said. "If you'd have said something was lit in my day, I'd have thought you meant drunk."

I merely smiled. It was weird having someone join in a conversation that the other parties to the conversation couldn't see or hear.

"Oh, my gosh!" Taylor stepped out from behind the Oriental screen and spotted the sketch. "Do you have this dress?"

"Not yet. Right now, it's still in the concept stage," I said.

"Hannah would look really pretty in that," Taylor said to Olga. "Don't you think?"

"Hannah is her best friend," Olga supplied. "They've been besties since Kindergarten."

"Taylor, if you or any of your friends would like to design your own dress, come by and we'll look at patterns."

"For real?"

I smiled. "For real." I handed both Taylor and Olga a couple of business cards. "And if you need photographs, the gorgeous guy upstairs can hook you up."

"He is gorgeous," Olga said. "I saw him on Saturday."

Taylor was talking excitedly to her grandmother as I walked them out. I felt sure the two of them—and maybe Hannah and some of Taylor's other friends—would be back. As Olga and Taylor went out the front door, Mark's mother and her psychic friend, Sabine, came into Shops on Main.

I greeted the women and then glanced toward the stairs. Mrs. Meacham wouldn't be happy if Sabine was here to try to conjure up Mark.

Sabine held her arms slightly out from her sides and closed her eyes. "I feel a strong presence here." She opened her eyes and brushed past me into Designs on You.

Lorinda and I followed Sabine. Lorinda looked hopeful that the presence was that of her son. I was concerned because I knew it wasn't. I was looking at "the presence," who was standing in the center of the room looking skeptical.

Sabine drifted near the spot where Max was standing.

"Can you see her…or him?" I asked.

Max used her fingers to make herself a set of glasses and poked her tongue out at Sabine.

Before I could stop it, I choked out a laugh that sounded like a seal's bark. Sabine turned and gave me a sharp look.

"I'm sorry," I said. "This just makes me nervous."

"I don't believe you need to be frightened of this presence," said Sabine. "I do not see it, but I don't feel as if it's malevolent."

"Is it Mark?" Lorinda whispered.

"No." Once again, Sabine closed her eyes. "This is a woman…a woman who lived here long ago."

Max turned her mouth down at the corners. "All right. What else ya got, Toots?"

"I believe the woman died here," Sabine said. "Perhaps in this very room."

"Close," Max said, "but no cigar." She pretended to smoke a stogie.

"If this isn't where the woman died, then this could be the room where she took ill…or could have even been poisoned."

At Sabine's words, Max looked shocked and then disappeared. I gasped. *Where had Max gone? Would she ever be back?*

"I don't care about some random woman who lived and died here," Lorinda said. "I want to know about Mark."

"Of course." Sabine turned and led the way into the hall.

Lorinda and I trailed behind Sabine, but I turned back around to see if Max had reappeared. She hadn't.

Connie had come to stand in her doorway, and her eyes met mine. There was a distinct question in Connie's eyes, and I shrugged. I certainly didn't have any answers at the moment.

"Althea, I'll be right back," Connie called to her customer. "I just have to run upstairs for a second."

I followed the three women to the bottom of the staircase but stopped and looked back toward my shop.

Max materialized at my side. "Go on back to Designs on You. I'll tag along and fill you in."

"I'm glad you're here."

Sabine overheard and thought the comment was directed at her. "Thank you, my dear, and remember, you have nothing to fear—not from Mark, if he's here, and not from the female presence I felt in your shop."

"Thank you." I went back to Designs on You. I didn't want to miss anything, but I didn't want to get on Mrs. Meacham's bad side my first day there either.

As soon as I got seated in front of my new sketch, Frank popped in through the door leading to the kitchen.

"Hi," he said. "Ella sent me to find out what's going on."

I told him as much as I knew. "I don't think they're going to conduct a séance or anything. I think Sabine just wants to see if she can feel Mark's presence upstairs."

"Lucky for them, Melba isn't here. She'd probably have a fit." He shrugged. "I don't care what they do, as long as they leave me out of their hooey. By the way, anytime your grandpa brings chicken and dumplings, let me know...but on the sly. Ella thinks hers are the best, but she's a lousy cook. Dave has her beat all to pieces...but don't say I told you so."

Max returned several minutes later.

"So, what happened?" I asked softly.

"Well, Mark's mother introduced herself to Jason. And—get this—Janice picks up her purse, locks her door, and leaves!"

"Just like that?"

"Exactly like that. She didn't say a word to anyone and left out the back," Max said.

"Wow. What did Jason say to Lorinda?"

"He offered his condolences and then waited to see what she wanted. He's ever so classy, you know. I think you two might be a really good match."

I let that comment slide. "And what did Lorinda say?"

"She asked Jason if Sabine could come into his studio to see if she could feel Mark's presence since it had previously been his office. Jason said, sure, Sabine came in, and she didn't feel a thing. I even went over to the other side of the hall so Sabine wouldn't be confused by feeling my presence there."

"And she didn't even detect that you were there?"

Max shook her head. "She said it's her strong belief that Mark has moved into the light because his presence isn't here. And I told you that last week."

"Yeah… Is Lorinda okay?"

"As much as she can be, I suppose. She's relieved that Mark's spirit is at peace, but she still wants justice for her son. Sabine said—and I quote—"I can tell you one thing. Your son died because of someone else's secret. But that secret will soon be revealed.'"

Chapter Ten

G randpa Dave's chicken and dumplings had been simmering on the stove in case anyone wanted some. Now I walked into the kitchen and switched off the burner, so the dish would be cool enough for me to wash it and take it with me when I went home. I saw that there wasn't much left. Remembering Ford saying how much he liked chicken and dumplings, I decided to take them to him. I spooned the contents of the pot onto a paper plate. I snagged a plastic fork from the box on the counter and took the plate upstairs to Ford.

When I got up there, I was relieved to see that his door was open. I was carrying the plate in both hands, and I was glad I didn't have to risk dumping it onto the floor when I knocked.

"Is that what I think it is?" he called.

"It is, if you think it's the last of Grandpa's chicken and dumplings."

"Let me clear a spot." Ford moved the books he was going through to the side.

Gayle Leeson

I put the plate on the cleared area and handed him the fork.

"I warn you, I might be a harsh judge. Granny's were the best I've ever had." He tasted the dish, arched a brow, and took another bite. "This is almost as good as what Granny used to make." He looked toward the ceiling. "I said 'almost', Granny!"

I laughed. "I'm glad to hear it. Grandpa Dave will be proud."

"He should be. How are you enjoying your book?"

"I love it. It's one I can read over and over again," I said.

"Me, too." He squinted, as if trying to remember. "'The cloud of caring for nothing, which overshadowed him with such a fatal darkness, was very rarely pierced by the light within him.'"

"That's wonderful! I'm afraid I can't quote anything but the opening lines...but everyone knows those."

"Not everyone, and I'm sure you're selling yourself short. You probably recall more than you think you do."

"I'd better get back to the shop."

"Thanks again for the chicken and dumplings," said Ford. "They're delicious."

"You're welcome." I went across the hall, tapped on Jason's door, and when he called for me to come in—a bit warily, come to think of it, I poked my head just inside.

"Hi. I just wanted to let you know I'll be ready to leave in a bit."

He grinned. "I'm ready to go now, but I suppose we should wait until quitting time. I'll be down at five on the dot."

"Great. See you then."

Janice gave a drawer in her shop a slam, causing me to start. I looked up to see that Janice's door was open and that she was scowling at me. I merely waved and hurried downstairs.

I went into the kitchen and washed Grandpa Dave's pot before returning to Designs on You. I sat the pot on the worktable beside my purse and noticed that Max was pacing the room.

"Oooh, she makes me so mad."

"Who?" I asked.

"Janice. That look she gave you! And could you feel her eyes boring into you as you walked down the stairs?"

"No."

"Well, they did. The pillowcase walked to the doorway just so she could watch you."

I grinned and took a page from Max's playbook. "Then I hope I gave her a good show."

Max laughed. "Well, I'm sure you did."

"Could've been better had I felt those eyes boring into me. But why would she be glaring at me?"

"Because you, Cinderella, are going to the ball while the stepsister stays home and makes jewelry." Max made a growly sound. "Can I trip her? Not down the stairs or anything…but enough to make her skin her knee or something."

"I don't know. Can you?"

She tipped back her head and looked up at the ceiling. "No. I tried once and couldn't."

A shocked and amused chuckle escaped my lips. "Are you kidding?"

Max leveled her gaze back at me.

"No, of course, you're not," I said.

"By the way, as soon as you're finished with *A Tale of Two Cities*, I'd like to read it. Hearing Ford quote it was intriguing."

"I can get you the ebook on the tablet, and we can read it at the same time."

"Well, now you're on the trolley!" Max clapped her hands. "We can have our very own book club for two."

"We certainly can." I went into the reception area, sat at the desk, and loaded the ebook onto the tablet. I turned to Max. "There you go."

When I got up, Max sat down and began reading. "This is great. Thank you."

"Anytime." I went back into the workshop and called Grandpa Dave.

"Hi, Pup."

"Hi, Grandpa. Did you go by and feed Jasmine?"

"I did you one better than that—I brought her home with me and fed her here. We had a terrific time batting around a foil ball until Jazzy knocked it under the refrigerator."

"Been there. I keep thinking that one day there will be such an ocean of foil balls under ours at home, that the refrigerator will get pushed out into the middle of the floor."

He chuckled. "If you aren't up to coming and getting Jazzy after your date, I'll bring her to you tomorrow. Of course, if you are up to it, you can come get her and tell us both all about it."

"All right. I'll let you know. Thank you...for everything."

"You're welcome for everything."

"I'm going to make some cards tonight to go on the doors asking people to please keep them closed so that Jazzy can be here with me." I paused. "Do you think that'll be all right?"

"I think it'll be fine."

"Ford liked your chicken and dumplings, by the way. He said they were almost as good as his grandmother's."

"High praise...but what's really on your mind?"

He knew me too well.

"Lorinda, Mark's mother, and her psychic friend Sabine were here today. Sabine seemed to detect Max's presence." I went on to tell Grandpa Dave about the encounter. I left out the part about Sabine insisting that someone's secrets were responsible for Mark's death.

"Did you and Max discuss what Sabine said about her?"

"Not really. It seemed to make her uncomfortable. In fact, she actually disappeared for a few minutes."

"If talking about her death makes Max uncomfortable, then we shouldn't bring it up, Pup. She'll tell us what she wants us to know if and when she wants us to know it."

"I know." Of course, I knew that. But I supposed Grandpa Dave was still acting as my teacher and mentor.

A few minutes after I spoke with Grandpa, Max came into room.

"I couldn't help overhearing part of your conversation with Dave," she said softly. "I'm not uneasy talking about my death with you or Dave...but I was perturbed when Sabine was poking into my life...or death...or afterlife." She lifted and dropped one shoulder. "Sabine isn't a friend. To her, I'm merely a 'presence'...not even a person."

"I understand." Although I had never thought about things from a ghost's point of view before, it made perfect sense.

"Something she said, though, about getting sick in the parlor—or, rather, your reception room—triggered a memory," said Max. "My friend Hazel Lowry came by with a bottle of bootleg liquor she'd gotten from her cousin in Knoxville the evening of my…fall. She and I had a shot of courage before getting ready for the dance."

"Could the liquor have made you sick?"

"I suppose it could've. More likely it made me drunk."

I made a mental note to see if I could find anything on Hazel Lowry.

Jason took me to Milano's Italian Cuisine. The hostess seated us in a tall wooden booth in the corner. The waitress arrived and took our drink orders.

When she returned with the drinks, we ordered—chicken Bianco for me and meatball Parmesan for Jason. As the waitress retreated, Jason raised his glass.

"To your successful first day."

I raised my glass and gently tapped his. "And to your first day in your new location. Did all your clients find you without any problem?"

"They did. All my appointments arrived on schedule. I even had a couple of unsettling walk-ins."

"Right. Mark's mom and her psychic friend."

"How'd you know?" he asked.

"They stopped in at Designs on You because Sabine felt a presence there. Lorinda hoped it was Mark, of course, but Sabine said it was a woman who'd lived and died in the house."

"Yikes. Did that freak you out?"

"No." I sipped my soda. "Sabine said the woman was friendly."

"So, she says you've got the female equivalent of Casper, and my studio gets the all-clear from the psychic even though a guy was murdered there. Makes sense to me."

"Do you think she's wrong? Did you get the feeling today that Mark was...well...there?"

"No. I don't believe in the supernatural. If I did, I'd have never leased that space." He inclined his head. "What about you? Do you believe in ghosts?"

I answered carefully. "I think there are definitely things in this world that we can't explain, so I try to keep an open mind. I'm more concerned about Sabine saying that someone's secret was the cause of Mark's death."

"They told you about that?"

Well, they hadn't, but I made a sound I hoped would come off as an affirmative.

"Don't let Sabine worry you. Her telling everyone standing around upstairs that someone's secrets—that someone apparently being a fellow Shops on Main vendor—led to Mark's murder was purely a theatrical scare tactic," said Jason.

"A scare tactic?"

"Yeah. Maybe she hoped to elicit a confession. Or maybe she was simply throwing it out there for Lorinda's benefit." He shrugged. "Or she could even be working for the cops to plant the suggestion in the killer's mind that they're on to him or her, if the police suspect the killer is indeed a vendor."

"Gee, I hadn't thought of that."

"Anything's possible," he said. "I do think it's good that Sabine told Lorinda that she felt certain that Mark's spirit had moved on into the light. Some spiritualists or mediums would have bilked the poor woman out of her life's savings in a quest for answers."

The waitress arrived with our salads. After she'd left and we'd drizzled salad dressing over our plates, Jason took the opportunity to change the subject.

"Did you grow up around here, Amanda?"

"I did. I still live in the house I grew up in, as a matter of fact. My parents moved to Florida, and I got custody of the house." I speared a piece of tomato. "What about you?"

"I grew up not too far from here in Morristown. I got a BFA in photography from ETSU, and then I took a year of wages saved from working part-time at a grocery store and traveled the country."

"That sounds exciting. Where did you go?"

"Louisiana, Texas, Oklahoma, Colorado, Wyoming, and Montana." He grinned. "It was great. I was basically a freelance photographer then. I'd send shots with interesting captions or anecdotes to magazines that would accept unsolicited submissions. I got more work from the editors who liked and accepted my initial photos. I enjoyed it."

"Do you still freelance?" I asked.

"Some. But my dad isn't in the greatest health, and I can't travel the way I used to. So I opened a studio in Johnson City."

"And that's where the location wasn't so good, right?"

"Good memory…and absolutely right. So here I am in Abingdon."

I smiled. "I'm glad."

"Me too."

The waitress brought our food, and I realized we'd barely touched our salads.

"Would you leave the salads please?" I asked.

"Sure. May I bring you anything else?"

"No, thank you."

Movement by the door drew my attention. "Oh, hey, that's Connie!" I looked at Jason. "You know, from Delightful Home, the shop across the hall from mine."

Connie was with a tall, barrel-chested man with sandy hair. He was dressed in a polo shirt and khakis.

"I think her husband is with her." I was glad. Connie was such a charming free spirit. It would be interesting to see what her husband was like. Was this a case of opposites attract maybe?

Connie glanced around the dining room, and I raised my hand to wave. Connie's eyes widened, she turned, took the man's arm, and propelled him from the restaurant, leaving the hostess gaping in confusion.

My jaw dropped. What was that about?

Jason turned to look. "I don't see them."

"They...um...they left."

Chapter Eleven

Jason dropped me back off at my car at Shops on Main after our date. Ever the gentleman, he waited until I got into the car and started it before he left me. I drove to Grandpa Dave's house to pick up Jazzy and to tell him about Connie.

"It was weird," I told him, once we'd both settled onto the black leather sofa in his living room. "I know she saw me, but she simply turned around and left."

"What did the man look like?" Grandpa asked.

I described the man I'd seen. "Of course, I only caught a glimpse of him before Connie hustled him out of Milano's."

He shook his head. "That doesn't sound like Connie's husband. I met him early this morning when I went to measure the cabinets. Will is of average height--about five feet, nine inches tall--and has reddish blonde hair."

"Was he nice? I mean, maybe the man with Connie was a divorce lawyer or something."

"Will was extremely nice. And he and Connie appeared to be very much in love."

"Well, I don't think it was someone she was having an affair with," I said. "Nobody would go to dinner with her lover in her own home town where she's likely to run into someone she knows."

"The simplest explanation is that Connie was meeting with the man to discuss some sort of business. She took a quick look around the restaurant, maybe realized it was too crowded to have a private conversation and decided to go elsewhere. I doubt she even saw you."

"I don't know... I could've sworn she saw me."

"Ah, Pup, I'm afraid that Mark's murder has you finding intrigue around every corner. If you're that curious, ask Connie about the incident tomorrow morning."

As I drove home, I realized that Grandpa Dave was right. I probably was skeptical of everyone and everything right now because of Mark's murder. I liked Connie and felt she was truly a sincere person. So, there should be a logical answer to why she'd behaved as she did at the restaurant tonight.

I wanted to trust everyone at Shops on Main but being naive could get me killed. After all, there was a strong possibility that one of my co-workers had already committed one murder.

I took a bath, slipped on some comfy pjs, and snuggled into my bed with my laptop. I was curious about Max's friend Hazel Lowry. When I performed an internet search, I was surprised at how many Hazel Lowrys there were, even when I narrowed the search by including the town. I added a timeframe and I found an obituary for a woman who could've been Max's friend--she'd have been about Max's age in 1930, and she'd lived in Abingdon.

The obituary said that Hazel had gone blind in May of 1930. That would have been around the time of Max's death. Since Max didn't say Hazel was blind, I was guessing that Hazel went blind after Max fell down the staircase.

The article went on to say that Hazel had been in poor health for the remainder of her life following her blindness. Date of death was August 28, 1932. She was survived by her parents and her younger brother.

How sad. I thought it was too weird a coincidence that Max had died and Hazel had gone blind at around the same time. What had they both been exposed to?

On Tuesday morning, I bundled Jazzy into her carrier, put the door signs I'd made into my tote, and headed for Shops on Main. Connie was waiting for me in the parking lot. She got out of her gray hybrid sedan and hurried over as soon as I'd located a space.

She knocked on the passenger side window. "Can we talk for a minute before we go in?"

"Sure." I unlocked the car.

Connie opened the door and slid into the passenger seat. Jazzy gave her a plaintive meow.

"Oh, that's right--you said you were bringing her today. Good." Connie smiled. "I wanted to explain why I didn't come over and talk with you last night at Milano's."

"You don't have to do that," I said. "Whatever was going on, it's your business, not mine." I tried to keep my voice from sounding judgmental. I didn't really feel judgmental about it--after all, I didn't know who the man was or why Connie was being secretive about seeing him--but I hoped she would decide to confide in me about it. She did.

"The man I was with was Janice's ex-boyfriend. I mean, Janice had still been stringing him along the whole time she was seeing Mark, but I suppose technically he's an ex. Anyway, my husband doesn't really like that I involve myself in other people's problems, especially these days. Will thinks my 'helping people' can be intrusive and ill-advised and, given Mark's death, even dangerous."

"He does have a point."

"I know, but I can't help myself. Poor Guy is simply head-over-heels for Janice. And he knows she's vulnerable right now and might need a shoulder to lean on."

"What advice did you give him?" I asked. "I mean, I might be missing something, but Janice doesn't seem that terribly brokenhearted to me."

"I agree. I'm afraid Mark might've thought the relationship was something more serious than it actually was." She shrugged slightly. "I told Guy to follow his heart."

"I guess you can't ever go wrong doing that, right?"

"Right." She checked her watch. "I guess we should get inside."

Connie didn't wait to walk with me, as I took Jazzy from the backseat. That was okay. I was ready to be alone with my cat...and with Max. I wanted to get Max's take on everything that had happened, mainly because I wasn't sure I was buying Connie's story.

Before even letting Jazzy out of her carrier, I put the signs I'd made on the doors requesting that the doors remain closed at all times to prevent Jazzy getting out of Designs on You. I didn't think she'd be particularly interested in leaving the shop, but I wasn't going to take any chances. After all, Shops on Main was a new environment for her, and she might be inclined to explore.

I didn't see Max right away, so after I got Jazzy settled, I went to the atelier. Jazzy hopped onto a windowsill and napped while I began working on another dress that I thought would be darling for a bridesmaid or prom gown. This one was patterned after the dress Rita Hayworth wore in the movie *You Were Never Lovelier*. I was going to make the dress in midnight blue and include the lace that ended on either side of the bodice as a shooting star.

"Good morning," Max said, appearing at my left elbow and peering at my sketch. "That's fabulous!"

"Thank you. How are you?" I inwardly cringed. That was a thoughtless question. I supposed I needed to break that habit.

"Still dead. You?"

"Still living." I grinned.

"How'd the date go?"

"Great!" I excitedly gave Max the details about my dinner with Jason. Then I told her about Connie.

Max tilted her head. "An affair, do you think?"

"I don't know. Grandpa Dave said she and her husband seemed very happy when he saw them yesterday morning."

"They do act all lovey-dovey when Will is here...and I've never seen Connie do the secret phone call thing Janice thinks she's so good at...but still..."

"It's weird."

"Very weird," she agreed.

There came a tap on the door, and then Connie popped her head inside. "Oh, you're working on a design. How cool!" She came inside to take a look at the sketch, and I saw that she was carrying a mug of tea. "I brought you a cup of kava." She placed the cup on my worktable. "May I?"

I nodded, and she picked up my sketchbook.

"Amanda, this is fantastic! You're such an artist."

"Thank you."

"Don't drink that tea," Max said.

"I...I appreciate that," I said, trying to ignore Max for the moment.

"This dress is gorgeous," Connie said. "Who is it for?"

"Whomever wants it." I smiled. "I thought it would be a lovely prom or bridesmaid dress."

"I don't know about bridesmaids--the women who wear this would outshine the bride." Connie chuckled and handed back the sketchbook. She lowered her voice. "Again, I'm sorry about last night. I just wanted to explain the situation before you met Guy, and I didn't want you to say anything to Janice about it in case he changes his mind and decides to find someone else-- which would be the best thing he could do."

"Right," I said.

"Anyway, I guess I'd better get back before some customer wanders in and thinks I've deserted the place." She left by the same door she'd entered. I was guessing she intended to make herself some tea.

"Do not drink that tea," Max repeated as soon as Connie had left.

"I'm not going to. Even though I think it's fine."

"You don't know that."

"No. I don't know that. I don't know anything. I don't know anyone here."

"You know me, kid. I won't steer you wrong. Someone in this place was murdered, and you and I are the only ones we know for sure didn't do it."

"There is that." I was eager to change the subject, so I told Max what I'd learned about her friend Hazel.

"Poor Hazel." She gave me a sad smile. "She was such a pretty, vivacious little thing. I hate to think of her blind and frail."

"It's too strange to be a coincidence, don't you think?" I asked. "You got dizzy and fell, and a few days later she went blind. Do you think there was something you were both exposed to?"

"All I know we were both exposed to was that hooch her cousin sent home with her from Knoxville."

Around eleven a.m., I was altering one of the ready-to-wear dresses for a lady who'd been in and bought the piece earlier. I told her I'd have the dress ready for her to pick up at lunchtime. There was a knock on my door, and before I could get from the atelier to the front room, two husky men walked into the room. One was dressed in jeans, biker boots, and a black t-shirt. The other wore greasy coveralls and work boots. Thankfully, they closed the door behind them; but since Jazzy skedaddled under the table near the window, I didn't have to worry about her running out into the hallway.

I was guessing they were in the wrong place, but I smiled and said, "Hello. Welcome to Designs on You. I'm Amanda. How may I help you?"

The man in the coveralls scowled as he glanced around the shop. "We're looking for Ford."

"Oh, yes. You'll want to go up the stairs and to your right. I was heading up there anyway. I'll take you." I wasn't heading up there anyway, but I thought I could say hello to Jason and maybe call the police if the men were here to beat up Ford or something.

I led the way out of my shop and closed the door. Then I walked up the stairs. One of the men fell into step behind me, and the other was at my side.

"You know Ford?" the man beside me asked.

"I do. I bought a copy of *A Tale of Two Cities* from him. What do you enjoy reading?"

"Lots of things."

Ford's door was open. I caught his eye and frowned as I glanced at the man beside me.

"These men are here to see you," I said to Ford.

"Great. Thanks, Amanda."

"I'm going over to Jason's office," I said.

"All right. See you later." Ford ushered the men inside and closed his door.

I didn't immediately hear any loud crashes or grunts of pain. Maybe the men were readers after all.

I tapped on Jason's door before popping my head inside.

"Hey, there." He looked up from his computer and smiled. "This is a nice surprise."

"Thanks. I was in the neighborhood…"

He chuckled. "I'm glad. Come on in."

I went inside and closed the door behind me. "I actually brought a couple of men up to Ford's shop. I thought they might be here to cause trouble for him or something, but they seemed to be all right."

"Rough-looking characters, huh?"

I nodded. "They didn't look like your typical Antiquated Editions customers."

"And what do typical Antiquated Editions customers look like?" Jason asked.

"Old people who like to read? Black horn-rimmed glasses perched on their skinny noses? Pocket protectors filled with expensive bookmarks?"

"No way." He scoffed. "They carry their expensive bookmarks in black velvet-lined cases."

"Oh, that's right!" I laughed. "Actually, I'm an Antiquated Editions customer."

"Then where are you hiding your horned-rims?"

"In my purse with my expensive bookmarks."

He stood and came around the desk. "I enjoyed last night."

"So did I. Thank you."

"Would you like to do it again sometime?"

"I would."

We heard voices nearing the door.

"That's my next appointment," Jason said. "I'll come down and talk with you in a little while."

"All right. See you then."

I left and was nearly at the bottom of the stairs when a man came into the building with a bouquet of red roses. I thought I recognized him as the man who was with Connie last night, but I wasn't certain.

"Pretty flowers," I said.

"Thank you." He brushed past me on the staircase. "Wish me luck."

"Good luck."

Ella hurried out of Everything Paper and craned her neck to watch the man's ascent. "What's going on?"

I shrugged. "That man came in with some flowers, asked me to wish him luck, and then hurried on upstairs. I guess someone has an admirer."

"I couldn't see him terribly well, but he looked like that man who used to date Janice." Ella scoffed. "Although I'm not sure Janice ever really cut ties with Guy, even when she was going out with Mark."

"I'd heard that Janice and Mark were seeing each other," I said. "But I thought they kept their relationship under wraps for some reason."

"They were trying to keep it from Mark's mother, who'd be beside herself to learn that her son was dating a woman not much younger than she. Everyone here knew what was going on though."

"Did that man who just went to take Janice a bouquet of roses know what was going on? I can't help but wonder if he did and if he's the jealous type."

Ella patted my shoulder. "Don't worry yourself overmuch about Mark's death. Frank and I believe we're safe here and that the person who killed Mark was a client. We let him upgrade our website for us." She clicked her tongue. "He not only overcharged us, but he did shoddy work." We believe that's why the police took all his files and his computer. They think it was a client too. Don't worry—they'll probably make an arrest any day now."

"I hope so."

I walked back into my office, ready to get back to work. Max was at the table talking softly to Jazzy.

"I'm sorry those palookas scared our sweet kitty," Max told me. "They did look like a couple of ruffians."

"They did. It usually takes a lot to ruffle Jazzy's feathers, but they sure got the job done quickly."

"I've been trying to find out more about what happened to Hazel, but it looks like other than reading and watching movies, I don't have the hang of this contraption yet." She nodded toward the tablet.

"We'll look for news on Hazel as soon as I finish these alterations, okay?"

"That's swell. Thanks."

Gayle Leeson

Max resumed the book she was reading while Jazzy lay curled up near her, and I went back into the workshop. As I worked, my mind wandered to the various people who had visited Shops on Main just this morning, and I wondered if we'd ever find out who killed Mark.

Chapter Twelve

I was working on my customer's dress alterations when Connie came into the front room.

"Hello!" she called.

"Back here."

She walked over to the sewing machine. "What are you working on?"

"A customer bought this dress earlier today, and she asked to have it tailored for her."

"Oh…that's great…isn't it?"

"It is," I replied. "If she's happy with my work, it's likely she'll be back."

"I don't see how anyone could not be happy with your work. Your designs are beautiful."

"Thank you."

Connie rolled a chair over so she could sit near me. "I saw Janice leave with Guy."

I nodded. "I saw him come in with flowers…red roses, as a matter of fact. He looked like he meant business."

"Yeah. I hope things work out for them, don't you?"

I simply shrugged.

Gayle Leeson

"What?" she asked. "You don't think they make a nice couple?"

"I don't know. I haven't even met him, and I'm barely acquainted with Janice," I said. "But it seems to me that she doesn't care about Guy if she was involved with Mark until...well, you know."

"True, but I don't believe Janice was ever all that serious about Mark."

"Maybe not, but it must've been serious to Mark. I mean, he talked with his mother about her."

Max appeared at my right shoulder. "Except he didn't tell Mommy dearest that his beloved was closer to the nursing home than she was!"

I lowered my head until I could hide my smile. I really did wish Max would stop popping up unexpectedly to provide commentary, no matter how amusing it was.

Connie sighed. "I can't help it. I want everyone to be happy."

"That's a noble goal," I told her.

Max snorted. "And about as likely as a pig growing wings and taking flight. Or me taking up knitting." She paused. "Do you think I could take up knitting?"

"I don't know," I murmured.

"About what?" Connie asked.

"About...about anything."

Connie patted my shoulder. "Poor dear. You've had a roller-coaster of an opening, haven't you?"

Ford opened the door leading to the workshop. "Hey, sorry for interrupting."

"No problem," I said. "What's up?"

"I'm going out for food and wondered if you guys would like anything."

"Nothing for me, thanks," Connie said. "I brought lunch from home."

"So did I."

Ford grinned at me. "Thanks for bringing my customers upstairs earlier, but I'm sure they could've found me on their own."

I looked down at my hands. "I was worried they were up to something. They didn't strike me as particularly scholarly types."

He laughed out loud at my comment. Then he said, "Hon, I'm sorry Mark's death got you off to such a rocky start at Shops on Main."

"I was just this minute telling her the same thing," Connie said.

"Well, I hope your fears won't cause you to leave. You've brought a breath of fresh air to the place."

"Thanks, Ford. I don't have any plans to go anywhere, but I do feel that we need to look out for each other."

"Excellent point." Connie put her hands on her elbows and hugged her arms to her chest. "We should do that no matter what. By the way, Ford, did the men Amanda brought upstairs buy anything?"

"One did—a 1960s collector's edition of Hemingway's *The Old Man and the Sea*."

"Ernie was a handsome bird, but I always preferred Fitzgerald's writing," Max said.

I was saying goodbye to Martha Brighton, the woman who'd bought the dress and had it altered, when Olga, Taylor, and a diminutive young woman Taylor introduced as Hannah came into Designs on You.

"I really want that green dress to wear to prom in the spring," Taylor said. "Only I want it in a bright pink. Can you do that?"

"Of course," I said.

Taylor shot Hannah a look of triumph. "Told ya. She can do anything."

"Well, I don't know about anything—"

"If I can find a dress I want, you can make it for me?" Hannah interrupted me.

"Most likely." I turned to Taylor. "Did you bring a fabric swatch with the color pink you have in mind?"

"No…but I'll know it when I see it. What have you got?"

I opened my laptop and logged onto a favorite fabric wholesaler's website. Taylor, Olga, and I looked through fabrics until we found Taylor's desired shade of pink in a bolt of chiffon. Hannah was too busy scrolling through her phone to pay much attention to us, but she gave Taylor an obligatory thumbs up.

I took Taylor and Olga back to the atelier where I took Taylor's measurements for the dress.

Hannah burst into workshop as I was measuring Taylor from the base of her neck to the center of her waistline. "I found it! I found my dress!"

I wrote down the measurement before looking at Hannah's phone. The dress she'd found was a white strapless gown accented with black embroidery. I immediately recognized it as the dress Hubert de Givenchy designed for Audrey Hepburn to wear in the movie *Sabrina*.

"Well?" Hannah stared at my face, her blue eyes sparkling. "Can you do it? Can you make this dress for me?"

"I can."

With a squeal, Hannah threw her arms around my neck and nearly knocked me down hugging me. I started to remind her that the dress wouldn't be cheap, but, of course, Taylor's dress wouldn't be either. If the girls didn't want one-of-a-kind dresses, they wouldn't be here.

Gayle Leeson

I finished Taylor's measurements, and Olga wrote me a check for the retainer. Hannah promised that she and her mom would be back on Saturday.

"Jolly good," Max said when we were alone in the shop. "You should be proud of yourself."

"I am." I sat on one of the wing chairs by the window.

Max appeared to sit on the other chair. "Then why don't you sound happier?"

"No reason. I suppose I'm just a little tired."

"Spill it. You know I'll find out eventually."

"Jason told me this morning that he'd be down to talk with me later today. I thought we were going to make plans to go out again."

Jazzy came over and hopped onto my lap. I stroked her short gray fur and was soothed by the sound of her purring.

"He's been fairly busy today," Max said. "Cut the poor man a little slack."

"I know he has work to do. I've had a lot to do myself." I blew out a breath. "I just don't want to get my hopes up where he's involved, you know?"

"Applesauce! The man likes you, or else he wouldn't have taken you to dinner last night."

"I know." I let my thoughts wander.

"You promised to help me find out more about what happened to Hazel," Max said.

"All right." I placed Jazzy onto the floor and went over to the desk where my laptop sat. I opened a new tab. "You said the only thing you two had in common was the liquor she brought from her cousin's house in Knoxville?"

"That's right."

I typed 1930 booze into the search bar and found articles by Time and Slate that suggested the alcohol was to blame for what had happened to both women. I was skimming one article, and then I turned to Max. "We don't have to do this."

"Yeah…please…I want to know."

The Time article pointed out that thousands of deaths per year could be traced to alcohol poisoning, but the really toxic substance that can end up in moonshine is methanol. I opened yet another tab and searched for methanol.

"Methanol, or wood alcohol, can lead to blindness, paralysis or death. Methanol metabolizes into formaldehyde in the body…" I stopped and scanned. "Max, it says here that the effects of methanol include fatigue, headache, nausea, vertigo, dizziness… That's what caused you to fall down the stairs."

"And what caused poor Hazel to go blind."

With a little more digging, Max and I discovered that the government added toxic ingredients to denatured industrial alcohols during Prohibition to make their consumption deadly.

We were still reading about "the chemists' war" in the 2010 Slate article when an older man ambled into Designs on You and sat on one of the navy wingback chairs.

The man turned his rheumy eyes toward me and smiled. "Hello."

"Good afternoon," I said. "Welcome to Designs on You."

He nodded toward the mannequin wearing the royal blue ready-to-wear dress. "My mother had a dress kinda like that one…quite a high-end garment, I imagine. Paid upwards of twenty dollars for it, if memory serves."

"I'm sure she looked beautiful in it."

"She did. I was awfully proud of her. She wore that dress when we went on the train. It was after Papa died during the war…in France." He looked off into the distance as if he were watching the events unfold on a movie screen. "We rode the Birmingham Special from Pennsylvania to Bristol…Mother, Roscoe, and I."

"I remember the Birmingham Special," Max said. "It was a passenger train that stopped at the Bristol Train Station. Mother, Dorothy, and I took that train to New York City once."

"Roscoe was four years old." The man continued his narrative. "I was six and thought I was the man of the house now." He chuckled. "A man at six. The things we get in our heads."

"It sounds as if your mother was a brave woman," I told him.

"She was. She truly was." He shook his head. "She once took Roscoe and me on a train and brought us all the way here from Pennsylvania to live with her family. We rode the Birmingham Special. It was after Papa died in the war."

I glanced at Max, who was looking a little sad at the man's retelling of his journey from Pennsylvania to Bristol. I felt sorry for him too.

Jazzy came over and rubbed around our visitor's ankles.

"What a pretty little thing you are!" he exclaimed. He patted his knees, and Jazzy obliged by hopping onto his lap. He stroked the cat's back for a moment before glancing at me. He did a double-take, as if he hadn't realized I'd been sitting there. "Oh…hello."

"Hello."

"I'm George."

"It's a pleasure to meet you, George. I'm Amanda."

"Is this your kitty?"

"Yes. Her name is Jasmine."

"She's very nice."

I smiled. "Thank you. She likes you."

"I like her too." He sniffed the air. "It's funny, but I don't smell the tobacco."

"Tobacco?"

"Yes. I thought this was a tobacco shop now."

"No," I said. "Fortunately for me, Mrs. Meacham leased the shop to me instead. I design and make women's clothing."

The door eased open, and a younger man stepped into the room. "There you are," he said to George.

"Roscoe! Come in and meet Amanda. She's turned the tobacco shop into a..." He struggled to find the right words. "A sewing room." He punctuated the end of his sentence with a triumphant nod.

I stood and extended my hand. "Hi, Roscoe. It's nice to meet you."

"Hey, Amanda." He shook my hand and lowered his voice. "It's Brett, actually. Brett Meacham. George is my grandpa."

George got up and tottered toward the atelier. "I want to find that tobacco...see if there's any cherry tobacco like we used to sneak from Granddad. Remember, Roscoe?"

"There's not any tobacco here, George." Brett quickly caught up to his grandfather and took him gently by the arm.

"Yes, there is. That good-for-nothing bum Mark has to go, and we're putting in a tobacco shop."

"But it's not a tobacco shop." Brett got in front of George, bent slightly to look the stooped man in the eyes, and spoke in a calm but firm tone. "This is a dress store."

George blinked a time or two. "Brett...what are we doing?"

"I brought you to see Grandma."

"Well, go up and get her, would you? I don't feel like climbing those stairs."

"All right." Brett helped George back to the navy chairs and helped him sit. He turned to me. "I'll be back in just a second."

"Sure," I said. "That's fine." I sat beside him. "I'm sorry we don't have any tobacco, George."

"I am too," he said. "But that Mark has to go. We're giving him the bum's rush because he won't pay his rent. We don't know what he's doing with his money...gambling or drugs is our best bet." He shrugged his bony shoulders. "You're a pleasant young lady."

"Why, thank you."

"You're very welcome. You remind me of my mother. She brought my little brother Roscoe and me here on the train way back in..." He screwed up his face. "I reckon it must've been '44 or '45."

"George!" Mrs. Meacham hurried into the room and took George by the hands. "Brett shouldn't have brought you out today. I think he got you over-excited."

"Nonsense, love." He smiled. "I was simply talking with this dear girl. She came here on the train...just like Roscoe and me."

"That's wonderful, sweetheart. Let's you and I go home. You can tell me all about it on the way."

"All right." George stood, told me goodbye, and said he hoped to see me again sometime. "Brett, I'll see you later."

"Okay, Grandpa. Have fun."

When Mrs. Meacham and her husband had left, Brett turned to me with a sheepish grin. "Sorry about that. Grandma thinks Grandpa should stay home and—how does she put it? —not get his feathers ruffled. But what a drag to be sitting around your house all day. Am I right?"

"I can see both sides," I said. "I understand that your grandmother wants to protect George, but I also feel that it's sweet of you to want him to keep enjoying life."

Brett sank onto the chair George had vacated and crossed his long legs at the ankles. "You're pretty patient. How many times did you have to hear that train story?"

"Oh, a time or two."

He chuckled. "Grandpa has his good days and his not-so-good days. This is one of the not-so-good. It was really hard to keep him out of the past today."

"I don't think the clothes helped much. I design clothing using retro patterns, so they have a vintage look."

"They're pretty." Brett's hazel eyes lingered on my face, and I could feel the color rising in my cheeks.

"What do you do, Brett? When you're not getting your Grandpa in trouble, I mean?"

"I'm a physical therapist."

I supposed that explained his physique. The man obviously kept himself in shape. I ignored Max giving him the once-over while I thought back to what George had said.

"I'm sorry your grandpa was so upset about the tobacco shop. Did he have his heart set on the shop going in here?"

"Who's to say?" He spread his hands. "It's like once something gets in Grandpa's head, it's hard to get it out. He must've heard Grandma say someone was thinking of putting a tobacco shop in the building, and now he thinks there's a tobacco shop here."

"What happened to the tobacco shop?" I asked. "I mean, I'm guessing I got this spot because I leased it first, but I thought the tobacco shop would go in where Mark's office was."

"Nope. The guy backed out entirely. I believe our resident bookseller might've had a hand in his decision."

"Ford? What do you mean?"

Brett shrugged. "You'd have to ask him about that."

"Your grandpa seemed fairly agitated about Mark Tinsley." I grinned. "'Give him the bum's rush'."

Brett got to his feet. "Yep, the old bum's rush. Don't pay your rent, you're out." He strode to the door. "It was nice meeting you, Amanda. I hope to see you again soon."

"You too."

"He seemed to be enjoying his visit until you brought up Mark," Max said.

"He did, didn't he? Do you think it's such a touchy subject because Mark was killed here?"

"Could be. Or it could be a touchy subject for an entirely different reason."

"Like what?"

"Like maybe he knows more about Mark—and his death—than he wants anyone to know."

Chapter Thirteen

I spent the rest of the afternoon waiting on customers—mostly browsers, but I had hope that at least one or two would return—and creating a muslin pattern for Taylor's prom dress. I learned the hard way when I made my first dress to always create a muslin to check the fit.

After work, Jazzy and I took burgers and fries to Grandpa Dave's house. While I put our dinner on paper plates and got out the condiments, Grandpa gave Jazzy a can of food.

"How was your day, Pup?"

"It was good...mainly. There were some odd moments." I told him about George Meacham observing one of my dresses and then telling me about his mother bringing him and his brother down from Pennsylvania on the train when he was a little boy. "He was so sweet, but it was sad. And he kept looking for the tobacco shop. I think he wanted cherry tobacco."

"My dad smoked a pipe and used cherry tobacco." He smiled slightly. "To this day, whenever I smell it, it takes me back to my old homeplace."

"Mr. Meacham's grandson Brett had brought him to Shops on Main, and Brett told me that Ford had dissuaded the tobacco merchant from opening his store there. Do you think that's true?"

"I don't know. I've only met Ford a time or two, and although he seems like a nice fellow, I wouldn't want to get him riled up at me."

"No...me either. Still, if it is true, why would Ford care who opened a shop in the building as long as it wasn't directly competing with his bookstore?"

"I don't know, Pup. If you're that curious about it, ask him."

"I will," I said. "That is, if I can come up with a way to do it diplomatically."

"You're nothing if not a diplomat." Grandpa Dave gave me a wink before biting into his burger.

"Max and I noticed that when I asked Brett about Mark Tinsley, Brett said his goodbyes and left. We thought that was a tad suspicious."

He wiped his mouth on a napkin. "You and Max are turning into a regular Nancy Drew and Bess, aren't you?"

"It's mainly Max. She's eager for us to solve this crime." I sipped my soda. "I have to admit, though, I'd feel a lot better knowing Mark's killer was behind bars."

"I don't want you working somewhere you don't feel safe. I'll be happy to help you find another location."

"No...not yet, anyway. I really like the shop, and..."

"And you don't want to leave Max," he finished.

"Well, yeah. I've never known anyone like her," I said. "Oh, by the way, Connie told me this morning that the man she was with at the restaurant was Janice's ex-boyfriend who was asking for advice. She ducked out of the restaurant because she didn't want her husband to know she was helping him. Connie says her husband thinks she's too involved with other people's problems."

"You sound as if you don't buy that story."

"I do...it was just weird, that's all. Guy—Janice's ex—did show up later with flowers, and I think he took Janice to lunch."

Grandpa Dave studied me as he stuffed a fry into his mouth. "What aren't you telling me?"

"I don't know. I just feel aggravated at myself because I don't even know Janice but was so willing to jump to conclusions about her."

"Like what?"

"Like believing she has loose morals because the man she was dating was murdered and two days later, Max and I could hear her heels clippity clopping across the hall to Jason's studio every little bit. And now this guy...Guy...shows up."

"But, as you pointed out, you don't really know Janice. And Max might tell you that you're basing your conclusions on circumstantial evidence," Grandpa said.

I shrugged. "I doubt it. She doesn't like Janice...and she's known her from the start."

"Observing and knowing are two different things." He chuckled.

"Maybe I'll go up and check out Janice's shop sometime tomorrow. At least, I could make an effort to get to know her."

"There you go. After we finish eating, would you like to play a game of rummy before you head home? Or do you and your young man have plans?"

"I'd love a game of rummy...and I don't have a young man."

"Well, what do you call a beau these days?" he asked.

"I'm calling Jason a friend." I took a big bite off my burger, so my mouth would be too full to answer Grandpa Dave's next question should he ask one. Fortunately, he didn't.

I went into work early the next morning hoping to catch Janice before customers began streaming in. Janice wasn't there yet, but Mrs. Meacham was in her office. After letting Jazzy out of her carrier and into Designs on

You, I went upstairs to the office. I tapped on the door, and Mrs. Meacham told me to come in.

"I don't want to disturb you," I said. "If this is a bad time, I can come back."

"This is fine. What's on your mind?"

"I wanted to tell you it was a pleasure meeting your husband and grandson yesterday."

Mrs. Meacham blew out a breath. "I'm glad. I was actually afraid you were coming to back out of your lease. I know there have been a lot of crazy things to deal with for having been here such a short amount of time."

"I don't plan on going anywhere." I smiled. "I enjoyed talking with Mr. Meacham."

"How many times did he tell you the same story?"

I glanced down at my folded hands. "Three."

"Which one?"

"The story about his mother bringing him and his brother to Bristol on the train."

"Ah, yes, the Birmingham Special." Her eyes grew misty. "I wish you could have known George when he still had all his faculties. He was as sharp as a whip, so very observant, and such a strong leader that people would follow him anywhere."

"From what little I spoke with him, Mr. Meacham appeared to have led an adventurous life. He made me wish the passenger trains were still running in Bristol. Wouldn't that be fun?"

"Fun? Travelling from Bristol to New York on a train?" She wrinkled her nose. "Not to me. Frankly, I prefer to stay at home. Travel is too much of a hassle anymore…at least, it is for me."

"Well, I need to get back downstairs." I stood. "I just wanted to tell you how much I enjoyed meeting Mr. Meacham and Brett."

"I'm glad…and I know Brett means well, but it disorients George when Brett takes him out galivanting."

I heard the clip-clop of heels and the jangling of keys in the hallway that cued me in to the fact that Janice had arrived.

"I'll talk with you later, Mrs. Meacham. I'm going to check out Janice's jewelry before I head back to Designs on You."

"Could you ask her to come over for a moment please?"

"Of course."

I stepped across the hall and greeted Janice.

"Hello." She sounded bored…or maybe tired.

"I'm finally getting up here to see your jewelry," I said. "Oh, and Mrs. Meacham wants to talk with you when you get a chance."

"Oh." She rubbed the back of her neck. "Um…well, you go ahead and look, and I'll…I'll see what she wants. Hopefully, this won't take long." She clickety-clicked across the hall.

I walked slowly around the shop. Many of Janice's pieces were the same but in different colors. For instance, there were tassel earrings made using red, black, white, yellow, pink, green, and orange beads.

"She keeps the good stuff in there."

I started at the sound of Max's voice. "You're going to give me a heart attack one of these days." I looked at where Max was pointing. It was a round table in the center of the room. There was an ornate necklace on a mannequin in the middle of the table. "Over there?"

"In the drawer."

I noticed that the table did indeed have a drawer. I went over and opened it. Inside there was a red velvet pouch. I opened the pouch and found a sapphire and diamond bracelet. Of course, it was bound to be fake, but it was lovely. I slipped it onto my wrist and held out my arm to admire it.

"This is gorgeous."

"You have excellent taste, kid. That's Tiffany."

Before I could disagree with Max, I heard Janice sputtering from the doorway, "T-take that off!"

"I'm sorry. I—"

"The p-pieces in that drawer are not for s-sale! Y-you shouldn't have been nosing through my things!"

"I didn't mean to." I took off the bracelet and returned it to the pouch. Then I apologized again, handed the pouch to Janice, and hurried downstairs.

As soon as I closed the door to Designs on You behind me, I looked at Max. "What just happened?"

"I was about to ask you the same thing. What got that old pillowcase into such a lather?"

"I suppose I shouldn't have opened the drawer, but if the pieces were that important—or not for sale—then she should've had them somewhere else. Right?"

"I agree a hundred percent. I truly thought that was where Janice kept the stuff she saved for her special customers or something."

I raised my brows. "I'm obviously not a special customer." I sank onto one of the navy chairs by the window. "That was a gorgeous bracelet though."

"I'm telling you—it's Tiffany. Excellent quality."

"I'll see if it's on their website." I got up, went to the desk, and opened my laptop. "I'm sure I can't afford it, but it might make us laugh to see how much the bracelet is selling for." I sat down and booted up the Tiffany & Co. website.

I scrolled through page after page of bracelets, but I couldn't find one like the bracelet Janice had in the drawer.

"I think you might be mistaken," I told Max. "There's nothing like that on the website."

She shook her head. "I know my onions when it comes to jewelry. Maybe the company only lists the newer designs on the website. That one is nearly as old as I am."

I scoffed. "No way."

"Okay, maybe it isn't as old as I am, but it's pretty old. My Aunt June had one just like it. We all loved Aunt June, but Dot and I were a little envious of all her jewelry. That woman was loaded. But she always gave us her cast-offs, so that was nice. We never got our mitts on that Tiffany bracelet though."

"Wait...you really think that bracelet upstairs is a real Tiffany & Co. piece from the 1920s?"

"Yeah...or thereabouts."

I searched for antique Tiffany bracelets and found one similar to the bracelet I'd discovered in Janice's shop. My jaw dropped when I saw the price tag--$85,000.

We heard Janice's heels clicking down the stairs, and I closed the laptop. She gave a perfunctory knock and then came into the shop.

"Hi." She gave me a smile that was a mere notch above a snarl. "I'm sorry I acted so crazy upstairs. It's just that...well, after having my shop vandalized and everything—"

"Oh, my goodness, I didn't even think of that!" I interrupted. "I really am sorry I opened the drawer."

"Nonsense. There wasn't any reason for you not to. It's just that the pieces in that drawer are custom items done for a particular client."

"I understand. That bracelet was beautiful. How much would you charge to make me one like it?"

Janice's eyes widened. "What? Oh...I...um...the custom pieces are guaranteed to be one of a kind."

"That's all right. I'd love to have one that's similar. I wouldn't expect an exact replica anyway."

She bit her lip. "Of course. I'm...um...backlogged right now...absolutely swamped, as a matter of fact...but I'll let you know when I'm caught up, and we'll talk about it."

"Okay. That'd be terrific. Thanks."

"See you later!" Janice left.

I turned to Max as we heard Janice clomping back up the stairs. "What do you think?"

"I think if that pillowcase ever made a bracelet anywhere near the quality of the one you found in that drawer then I'm Fanny Brice."

I smothered a laugh. "Why do you keep calling her a pillowcase?"

"Because her head is full of feathers. And yours is too, if you believe that baloney she fed you."

"No. She acted really weird...but why would she lie?"

"I don't know. But I'll see if I can't find out."

Before I could say anything more, Max was gone. I guessed she was off to spy on Janice. I wondered if I should feel guilty about that, but then I decided that I wasn't the one spying.

I was in the workshop sewing Taylor's muslin pattern when Jason came to see me. He brought a large canvas wrapped in brown paper.

"I have a surprise for you," he said.

"That's huge!"

"It's twenty-four inches by thirty-six inches—the perfect size to go over your mantle. Open it."

I carefully tore the paper away from the canvas and saw that it was the photo of me wearing the emerald evening gown and looking back over my shoulder at him.

"Shall we hang it?" Jason asked.

"Yes, please."

After we got the photo hung, Jason asked me if I was free for lunch.

"I'm sorry, but I'm afraid I can't today. I really have to get this pattern done."

"What about tomorrow?"

I smiled. "Tomorrow sounds good."

"Then it's a date."

He handed me a CD with the rest of the photographs from the shoot on it. Once again, I offered to pay him, and he refused.

As soon as he left, Max said, "Good move turning down lunch today. Play hard to get."

"I'm not playing anything. I really do need to get Taylor's muslin pattern finished."

Ford opened the door to the reception area and looked around before coming in. "Sorry...I thought I heard you talking to someone."

"Just Jasmine...the cat...I was telling her I don't have time to play right now."

He looked over at Jazzy, who was snoring softly on her bed. "Uh-huh."

"She likes to play...usually... Of course, she also likes to sleep. Like she is now. I guess I was just procrastinating." I barked out a little laugh. "Did you need me?" I asked.

"I was just going out for lunch and wondered if you'd like me to bring you anything."

"I appreciate that, but I'm fine."

"All righty."

"Before you go..."

He turned back. Was he looking wary, or was I imagining it? Of course, he did catch me talking to a sleeping cat, as far as he knew.

"I met George Meacham and Brett yesterday," I said.

"They're good people. George has gone downhill over the past year or so. I hate that."

"Yeah…Mrs. Meacham said this morning she wished I could've met him when he had all his faculties."

Ford nodded, and I got the impression I should say what I wanted to say because he was ready to leave.

"Brett mentioned that you opposed the tobacco shop," I blurted.

"And?"

"And…thank you." I smiled. "If that tobacco shop had moved in, I wouldn't be here."

"Well, then, you're welcome. I just didn't want my books to smell like tobacco."

With that, he left.

I turned to Max and said—in hushed tones this time, "Would tobacco smell get into books? I'd have thought that would only be the case if someone smoked in the same room with them."

"I don't know about that," Max said. "But you need to clam up from now on instead of trying to lie. The more you talk, the worse it gets. Dot was like you—that poor kid couldn't lie if her life depended on it. Me? I could lie like a rug in a well-traveled hallway."

Chapter Fourteen

Olga brought Taylor in after school. When I brought out the muslin, I thought Taylor was going to cry.

"This is only for your fitting," I assured her. "If we make any mistakes in fitting, we want to make them with this cheaper material rather than that of your actual dress. This muslin is what I'll use to create your actual pattern. And I can keep it on file for you in case you'd like another dress for a pageant or some other occasion."

Taylor let out her breath. "That's good. That makes sense."

"Your dress fabric isn't even here yet." I led her behind the screen to try on the muslin. "We only ordered it yesterday, and it won't be here for a few days. This muslin is simply to make sure I have the correct measurements."

"Gotcha." Taylor slipped out of her jeans and tee shirt and put on the muslin.

I needed to take it in a little more in the waist. I pinned the adjustment before allowing her to take off the garment.

When she emerged from behind the screen dressed in her school clothes again, she beamed at Olga. "It's gonna be perfect, don't you think, Grandma?"

"I do, angel. You'll be the prettiest girl at prom."

Taylor scoffed, but she was pleased by the compliment.

I didn't hear Connie walk across the hall in her rubber-soled sandals, nor did I hear her open the door, so I was mildly surprised when she walked from the reception area into the atelier.

"Hi, everyone." Her smile encompassed us all. "I was busy earlier but got over here as soon as I could. Did I miss the fitting?"

"Only of the—" Taylor looked at me.

"The muslin," I supplied. "It's to make sure the actual dress will fit just the way we want it."

"It's going to be gorgeous," Olga said. "She's going to be gorgeous. I mean, she already is, but—"

"Grandma!" Taylor rolled her eyes but squeezed her grandmother's shoulders in a one-armed hug.

Olga glanced at her watch. "We'd better run. I promised Taylor's mom I'd have her home before five."

"We've got time," Taylor said.

"Not if we stop by Anthony's and share an ice cream."

Taylor laughed. "See you guys later!"

"They're sweet," Connie said, as the pair left Designs on You.

"They certainly are." I could tell Connie had a specific reason for lingering, and I wished she'd get to the point.

She must've read my mind.

"Janice seemed to be in a tizzy earlier... I hope it didn't have anything to do with Guy."

"It had nothing to do with Guy and everything to do with me." I told her about being in her shop and opening the apparently forbidden drawer. "I'd have thought any special pieces would have been locked up somewhere, especially after her shop was ransacked."

"So would I. What did the bracelet look like?"

"It was incredible. It had sapphires and diamonds—fake, I'm sure—but it was elegant and done in an Art Deco style," I said. "Janice later came down and apologized for flying off the handle, and I asked her about the bracelet. She said it was a custom piece made particularly for one of her clients. I asked her to make one for me, but she said she was backlogged."

"Wait...Janice made this bracelet you found? The one in an elegant, Art Deco style?"

I nodded. "Why do you ask?"

"I've never known Janice to make anything overly complicated. And never a one-of-a-kind piece." Connie looked over her shoulder, as if doublechecking to make sure Janice hadn't come in and was hearing every word. "Don't get me wrong—her jewelry is nice enough…for what it is…but it isn't high-end stuff."

"This bracelet certainly was."

"And she told you she made it?"

"Yes."

"Huh…you learn something new every day, I guess." She shook her head as if to dismiss thoughts of Janice and her jewelry. "I'm glad things worked out with Taylor."

"Me too."

"I'm looking forward to seeing the finished piece." She wandered toward the door.

I wasn't sure if she was waiting for me to say something or what, so I thanked her again for introducing me to Olga.

"Oh, that's fine. That was all you and that gorgeous dress you were wearing." She glanced up at the mantle and did a doubletake. "Well, there it is! That's an incredible photograph."

"Thank you."

She gave me a wide smile. "I'd better get back. Talk with you later."

Max appeared at my side and watched her go. "She thinks we're all friends again, but I'm not so sure."

"Were we all ever not friends?" I asked softly.

"You didn't drink the tea, did you?"

"Well...no. But I was ridiculous not to...don't you think?"

She lifted and dropped one thin shoulder. "Who's to say? At this point, I'm going with the old better safe than sorry adage. Connie and I agree on one thing, though—Janice didn't make that bracelet."

"Then where do you think she got it?" I asked.

"I don't know." Max ran her index finger below her lower lip as she contemplated. "I do know this. After she came down here and said she was sorry for blowing a gasket, she went back upstairs, called someone, and said she wasn't comfortable keeping the pieces here anymore."

"Do you have any idea who she was speaking with?"

"No, but she said she didn't want the responsibility for the jewelry on her head."

"What did she do with the jewelry? Surely, she didn't put it back in the drawer where I found the pieces?"

"Yep, she did." Max shook her head. "Ridiculous. If she'd really wanted to hide the jewelry, she should've put it in one of Ford's old books."

I frowned, not following her logic.

She rolled her eyes, reminding me of the teenager who had so recently left. "Didn't you see those books Ford has with the middles cut out?"

"No!" I reminded myself to lower my voice. "Why would Ford have books with the middles cut out? Those are rare editions."

"I'm just telling you like it is, sister. The man cuts up some of those books so people can hide things in the middle."

"What kinds of things?" I asked.

"Depends on how big the book is, but I'd imagine you could stuff money or a pistol in one easily. And I know for sure that jewelry would fit. I mean, if Janice couldn't get it all in one book, it would fit in two, no problem."

"Wait." I ran my hand across my forehead. "You've actually seen Ford cutting up books? You're sure they aren't book safes?"

"Yes. They're books until Ford cuts the middles out of them and puts the discarded pages through the shredder. Then they are safes." Max spread her hands as if I was being particularly dense.

"Why would he do that?"

"Obviously, so somebody can hide something in the books."

"That doesn't strike you as odd?" I asked.

"People stopped trusting banks soon after I died. I know about my family going bankrupt. If I was alive today, I'd keep all my money in Ford's books."

"Banks are more secure these days."

She shrugged. "We thought they were secure then too."

"I'm starting to have serious doubts about setting up shop here." I wandered over, picked up Jazzy, and cradled her against my neck. She started to purr, a low, soothing rumble.

"You're having doubts about this place? Dollface, you're doing great here! I was honestly afraid you'd be off to a slow start. But news about your skills is spreading like wildfire, and you're doing aces."

I merely nodded.

About half an hour before closing time, the woman who'd been one of my first customers came in. She was the woman who'd accompanied her frenemy into the shop and then ran back inside to get a business card after "forgetting" her purse.

"Hi! It's great to see you again."

"It's great to see you. I don't think I told you my name the last time I was here. It's Ruby Mills."

"It's a pleasure to officially meet you, Ms. Mills."

She scoffed. "Please call me Ruby. Anybody who's going to wind up seeing me in my skivvies should call me by my Christian name."

"All right." I smiled. "I take it you're here about that dress for your granddaughter's wedding."

"You're absolutely right. Keen memory!" Ruby held her arms akimbo. "What can you do for me?"

I tilted my head as I considered her. "You're a petite pear shape, meaning your hips are wider than your shoulders, and you have a defined waist. We'll want to accentuate your shoulders and draw attention to your upper body and waist." I stepped over to the desk and grabbed a sketchpad and a pencil. "We'll also want to elongate your legs." I began sketching out an A-line dress with a wide scoop neck and three-quarter length sleeves.

"What about bows on the shoulders?" Max murmured.

I hadn't realized the ghostly fashionista was in the room, but I was too caught up in the dress design to be startled. And she'd made an excellent suggestion.

"I think Valentino did something similar with a sleeveless dress, and it was stunning," I said.

"Did what, dear?" Ruby asked.

"Um…bows on the shoulders." I sketched in the bows. "But since this wedding will take place in the fall, you'll want at least three-quarter length sleeves." I elongated the sleeves. "Still, I like the bows…do you?"

"I do." Ruby peered at my sketchpad. "It gives the dress some extra oomph."

"I like this woman," Max said.

"What color do you think?" I asked.

"Green," Max said.

"I don't know," Ruby answered.

"What color is the bridal party wearing?" I asked. "We don't want you to clash."

Max waved her arm around. "Clash...stand out...it's a gray area."

"The bridesmaids are wearing blue," Ruby said. "Or, at least, I hope they are. Right now, Heather, my granddaughter, says the gals are bickering like crazy over the dresses."

"Well, it's difficult to choose one particular dress that will be universally flattering." I led Ruby into the atelier so I could try swatches of fabric against her skin. "Hopefully, they'll find something they can agree on."

"Would you mind consulting with them?" Ruby asked.

"Not at all." I held a forest green bolt of crepe fabric beside Ruby. "You'd be breathtaking in this color, and it would complement any shade of blue nicely."

"All right." Ruby smiled. "Let's do it."

I got out my tape measure and took the necessary measurements. When we were finished, Ruby called her granddaughter. By the time Ruby left, I had an appointment to see Heather and her four bridesmaids at ten a.m. the next day.

"Good job!" Max said. "See? I told you not to get discouraged."

"You had some excellent suggestions. Thank you. But the reason I was discouraged wasn't because of business, it was because of...well, everything else."

"We'll figure out who murdered Mark soon enough. Then we're coasting."

I sat down to do a more accurate sketch of Ruby's dress. "I believe we should leave the investigating to the police."

"What? Are you off your nut? We know far more than the coppers. And we're in the perfect position to investigate."

"No, we aren't. We don't know anything. Everything we think we know is purely conjecture."

"That's why we need to keep investigating."

I concentrated on my sketch.

"I can't do it alone, or I would," Max insisted.

I gave my head a weary shake. When I looked back up, Max was gone.

My day had been one of extreme highs and lows, and when Jazzy and I got home, I felt drained. I gave her a can of food, and I had a peanut butter sandwich and some pretzels while I thumbed through a catalog that had come in the mail.

I tried to concentrate on the good—Taylor's muslin fitting had gone well, Ruby was pleased with her dress design, and Ruby's granddaughter and her bridesmaids were coming in to see me tomorrow morning. Still, the bad kept intruding.

Even if that bracelet and the other pieces of jewelry in the drawer at Janice's Jewelry were custom pieces, I couldn't understand why Janice would get so upset by someone admiring them. If I had a custom dress in the atelier at Designs on You and someone saw it and wanted one like it, I'd be flattered. And then I'd offer to make her a custom dress more suited to her personal style. I wouldn't be angry. It wasn't as if I'd opened Janice's purse. Had the jewelry supposed to have been kept somewhere private, then it shouldn't have been on the sales floor. I realized I was making excuses for myself, but I really didn't think I'd committed such a huge sin by merely opening a drawer and admiring a bracelet.

Max was positive that Janice hadn't made the bracelet herself, and Connie seemed to agree with that assessment. I, too, conceded that nothing else in Janice's Jewelry even came close to the workmanship of that bracelet. But if Janice hadn't made it, where had she gotten it, and why was she lying about making the bracelet? I'd never lie about making an Alexander McQueen should someone come into my shop and see one hanging in the workroom.

I played the conversation out in my head.

"Wow, did you make this?"

"No, it's an Alexander McQueen. Isn't it lovely?"

"Yes, I'd love one!"

"Well, you can try Neiman Marcus, or I can design something in a similar style for you."

I would never say, "Of course, I made it. But I'm too backlogged to make you one." Especially because making dresses is my business. Just like, I'd assumed, making jewelry was Janice's business.

As I washed down a bite of peanut butter sandwich with a drink of iced tea, I found myself wishing I could've gotten a look at the rest of the jewelry in that pouch. I wasn't sure quite why I wanted to see it, but I desperately did. Maybe it was to see if the quality of that one piece was a fluke. Or maybe, I wanted to know if these were expensive pieces that Janice had bought at an estate sale or something and hoped to pass off as her own. Still, I couldn't imagine Janice paying over eighty thousand dollars for a single bracelet. How would she ever make her money back on it?

And what about Ford and his hollowed-out books? Could Max have been mistaken about what she'd seen? Somehow, I doubted it. Max didn't appear to be mistaken about very much. Still, I couldn't imagine what Ford could be hiding. Or what he was helping someone else hide.

I sighed, took another drink of tea, and wondered if I should take Grandpa Dave up on his offer to relocate Designs on You.

Chapter Fifteen

I didn't see Max when I went into Designs on You on Thursday morning. I let Jazzy out of her carrier before stowing it in the atelier near her litter box, and I walked around both rooms.

"I'm sorry, Max," I said softly.

Still nothing.

I watched Jazzy. She sniffed around the mantle before hopping onto the chair behind my desk. The cat didn't seem to sense Max's presence, as she had before.

It wasn't unusual for Max to be absent, of course, but this was the first time we'd had a disagreement.

I wandered into the workroom, opened the filing cabinet, and thumbed through patterns until I found one I could use to make the muslin for Ruby Mills' dress.

I heard someone open the door to the reception area and stepped around the corner to see Melba and George Meacham.

George smiled and spread his arms. "Hello!"

"Good morning, Mr. Meacham. How are you?"

"Fine, thank you. How are you?"

"I'm well. Mrs. Meacham, how are you?"

"Rushed," she said. "George and I are on our way to his doctor's appointment, but I forgot something upstairs yesterday evening. Would you mind keeping George company while I run up and get it? I hate to make him climb the stairs."

"I'd love having a chat with Mr. Meacham." I took his arm and led him over to the wingback chairs sitting near the window. "Would you like some coffee or water or anything?"

"He can't have anything to eat or drink before his appointment," Mrs. Meacham said. "Be right back." With that, she hurried off to retrieve whatever it was she'd forgotten.

I sat on the chair next to Mr. Meacham.

He pointed to the mannequin wearing the ready-to-wear dress. "My mother had a dress like that. She wore it when she brought Roscoe and me to live here." He glanced at me sideways and gave me an impish grin. "Roscoe has sticky fingers sometimes. I never rat him out, but she's gonna catch him sooner or later, and then it'll be on."

"I bet it will. Our bad decisions can have a way of catching up to us, can't they?"

He laughed as he nodded. "One time, Roscoe stole Aunt Sue's prune Danishes. She didn't even know it was him until he got sick. I told him he shouldn't have eaten them all at once."

I joined in his laughter. "Did he even give you one?"

"Not even a bite."

"Served him right to get sick then, didn't it?"

Mrs. Meacham returned in time to hear the end of George's story. "That Roscoe was one incorrigible young man."

"Was he a bad influence on you, Mr. Meacham?" I asked.

"Nope. I'm the big brother. I don't let him sway me."

"We'd better go, dear." Mrs. Meacham came over and took her husband gently by the arm. She mouthed a thank you to me, and I nodded.

I made a mental note to ask her later if Roscoe was still living. If so, I hoped he was still in the area. I thought it might do Mr. Meacham good to visit with his brother. At their ages, Roscoe's incorrigible days should be far behind him.

Heather and her bridal party arrived at just before ten o'clock. Heather's sister Hailey was tall and willowy, like the bride. Heather's friend Laura was also tall, but she was curvy. Her cousin Simone was short with an athletic build. Heather's fiancé's sister Emily was average height and her pregnancy was showing…early-to-midway into the second trimester was my guess. I'd need to take her growing tummy into account with the dress design.

"We simply can't find dresses that flatter each of them, and I don't want to be one of those brides who makes her best friends wear unattractive bridesmaids' gowns," Heather said. "My grandmother thinks you're some kind of miracle worker, so…what can you do for us?"

"Well, let's see." I brought some chairs from the workroom and placed them around the desk in the reception room. I then pulled the navy wingback chairs over to desk so that the women could sit in a semicircle around my workspace. Then I gently removed Jazzy from her resting place on my desk chair. With a small meow of protest, she sashayed into the atelier.

I opened my sketchbook to a blank page and grabbed a pencil. "I believe that an empire waist with a deep vee neck and back with a full skirt is going to be the most universally complimentary." I roughed out the design as I spoke so they could see my idea as it was forming. "The dress should be crafted in tulle with a floor-length skirt. That way, no one will notice shoes." I glanced at Emily. "You could even wear sneakers if you want."

She laughed. "I might really do that!"

"To give the dress added elegance, I'd add silver beading at the waist to form something like an elongated medallion. It wouldn't go all the way around the waist." I drew it onto the dress. "It would merely be an accent piece...like this."

My gaze encompassed them all. "Of course, if you aren't happy with this design, I can try again."

"No," Heather said. "I think this is what we've been looking for." She looked at her friends for confirmation. "Right?"

They each assented.

"What do we need to do next?" Heather asked.

"Choose a color. I think Mrs. Mills indicated you wanted blue?"

She nodded.

"Then let's choose a blue." I took out a color swatch with the shade in several hues. They settled on Egyptian blue, a deep royal. "Shall we get everyone measured?"

Jason arrived to pick me up for lunch just after I'd finished measuring the last of the bridesmaids. I introduced him.

"This is Jason Logan," I said. "He's a wonderful photographer...and I speak from experience."

Heather followed my eyes to the portrait over the mantle. "You did that?"

He nodded.

"Could I have one of your business cards please?" she asked.

"Me too?" Emily stepped forward with one hand on her stomach. "I'm going to be needing some photographs before too much longer."

Jason handed cards out to all the women as they filed out the door.

"You know, you should leave some there on the mantle," I said. "You might not always make such a timely appearance."

"Good thinking. Are you ready to go?"

"I am. All that measuring has given me an appetite."

We went to lunch at Jack's 128 Pecan. It was a rustic place with lots of dark wood and where the fries were served in small terra cotta flower pots. How could you not love a place where the fries are served in flower pots? Jason had the fried green tomato and pimiento cheese sandwich, and I had the fried egg sandwich.

At first, we discussed the wedding party and how Heather's visit to Designs on You seemed to work out well for both of us.

"It seems like that woman who came in on your first day has brought a lot of business your way," he said.

"I know. That's great, isn't it? I'm really pleased with the way everything has been going." I shrugged slightly. "I know this is a feast or famine kind of business, but I'll enjoy the feast while I have it. What about you? Are you settling in well at Shops on Main?"

"I am. I was afraid there would be people wanting to come into my studio...you know..." He lowered his voice to just above a whisper. "Because someone died there. But I haven't had too many looky-loos."

"I never even thought of that. It's just so morbid. I'll be glad when the case is solved. It seems as if everyone is on edge—Connie, Janice..."

Jason shook his head. "You don't know how relieved I am that Janice finally stopped coming over to my studio every few minutes to ask for my help with this or that or to ask if I needed anything." He ate one of the Parmesan fries. "I'm all for being neighborly, but that was ridiculous."

"I think you know it was more than Janice trying to be neighborly."

"I do know." He laughed. "I think I finally got my point across when I told her how much she reminded me of my mom."

My jaw dropped. "You didn't!"

"I did."

We shared a laugh.

"Just be glad you stayed out of her drawers," I said.

He raised his eyebrows, and I realized how far I'd put my foot into my mouth. I could feel my face burning.

"Um...you see...I...yesterday, I opened a drawer in her shop and found a beautiful bracelet, and Janice had a fit." I explained how she came down later and said it was a special piece for a particular client. "But, still, I shouldn't have been...you know...messing where I had no business."

"You had no idea that a piece of jewelry in a jewelry shop was off limits. If the piece had been set aside for some reason, it should have been at least behind the counter."

"I agree." I was eager to get the subject off Janice's drawers. "So, what do you think of Ford?"

"I like him all right. He pretty much keeps to himself, so I don't know him all that well."

"That's been my experience too. Has Ella given you a ten percent coupon off at Everything Paper?"

"She has!" He grinned. "I'm saving it for something big."

"Me too."

When we returned to Shops on Main, I took the sign off the door telling potential customers I'd gone to lunch and inviting them to either come inside to wait or to call for an appointment. Jason went up to his studio and brought back a stack of his business cards in a Lucite holder.

"You're certainly prepared," I told him, as I placed the cards on the mantle beneath the portrait.

"I try. Do you have some cards to share with me?"

"Yes, but I don't have a holder for them."

"That's all right," he said. "I'll find a prominent place for them."

I gave him a stack of business cards and thanked him for lunch. "I really enjoyed it."

"I did too. Better run, though. I have a client coming in."

I smiled slightly as I heard his feet tromping up the stairs. I wandered into the atelier where Jazzy was lying on her bed looking up at Max, who was perched atop the filing cabinet.

"Did Mr. Wonderful buy you lunch?" she asked.

"He did."

"You should make dinner for him to return the favor. Men love that sort of homey thing. It assures them that if they wind up shackled to you for life, they won't starve to death."

"I'm glad you're back," I said.

"I never left."

"I'm sorry about yesterday." I spread my hands. "I was frustrated."

"I know. I spent the morning in Janice's shop. I got to see another piece from that pouch you found, and it's a Buccellati brooch."

"Buccellati?" I wasn't familiar with the name.

"Yeah." She winked. "Look it up."

We went into the reception area, and I did an Internet search for Buccellati. When I found a Buccellati brooch selling for over forty-five thousand dollars, I turned to Max slack-jawed.

"Are you sure the brooch upstairs is a Buccellati?"

"Positive. This time I saw the name on the back."

"We've got to find out the truth about that jewelry!"

Max gave an exaggerated nod. "And find out why the pillowcase is trying to convince us she made it."

"But how?"

"We'll both think on it," she said. "Hopefully, one of us will come up with something."

I was in the atelier cutting out Ruby Mills' muslin when Mrs. Meacham came into the reception area.

"Amanda, dear, are you here?" she called.

"In the workroom," I responded.

She briskly stepped into the atelier and surveyed the room before nodding with what I presumed was approval. "Thank you for entertaining George earlier. He likes you...calls you that pretty dressmaker."

"I was glad to do it. How did his appointment go?" I asked. "I hope he got a good report."

"He did..." She lowered her eyes. "For the most part."

"Is there anything that can be done for his dementia?"

"Not really. It's a cruel thief."

"He speaks often about Roscoe. Does his brother live around here?"

"No. He died in a factory accident when he was in his late twenties." Her words were clipped, and I got the impression she didn't relish talking about her brother-in-law.

"That's a shame."

"It is. But these things happen."

Despite getting the distinct impression Mrs. Meacham didn't care to discuss her husband's late brother, my curiosity got the better of me. "Does Brett resemble Roscoe? I only ask because Mr. Meacham called Brett by his brother's name when they were here the other day."

She pursed her lips. "That's how it is with George now. Sometimes Brett is Brett, and other times he's either our son Jack or George's brother Roscoe. I'm either Melba or Mother. We act as if we're whomever we're supposed to be at the time."

"I imagine that's the best course of action."

"I suppose. It's less confusing for George that way, and there's no point in arguing with him. Whatever he has in his mind is his truth at that moment. The rest of the family is forced to wait for—and treasure—those glimpses of lucidity." She presented a tight smile—obviously her version of a stiff upper lip. "Thanks again. I won't keep you."

"Anytime."

After Mrs. Meacham left, I started thinking about Grandpa Dave. I'd be heartbroken if he didn't recognize me and couldn't remember the times we've shared. I took out my cell phone and gave him a call.

"What's up, Pup?"

"I wanted to invite you over for dinner tonight. I thought maybe I'd get a pizza from Mamma Mia's."

"That sounds great. What time do you want me there?"

Max appeared on the workroom table right atop Ruby Mills' muslin pattern and let out a sigh that would've done any melodramatic actress proud. "I wish I could be there."

"Max says she wishes she could be there," I said. "Grandpa, would you care to have dinner here?"

"I'd love to! Tell Max I'm thrilled to have two gorgeous dates."

"Would you mind bringing a can of food for Jazzy?" I asked.

"Not at all. I can even go by and pick up the pizza."

"No way." I was emphatic. "Tonight's dinner is on me. But do bring the cards. Maybe we can play some rummy."

Max clasped her hands together. "I can hardly wait!"

Chapter Sixteen

Grandpa Dave was at Designs on You when I returned with the pizza. He'd already fed Jazzy, and he and Max were in a spirited discussion about *The Thin Man* movie. Everyone else had left Shops on Main, so after handing Grandpa the pizza, I went back to lock the front door and made sure the back door was locked as well.

When I walked back into the shop, Grandpa Dave had brought a couple of paper plates and napkins from the kitchen and had placed the pizza box on the round table between the wingback chairs.

"Is the coast clear?" Max asked. She was sitting on the desk and Jazzy was gazing up at her.

"I believe it is." I put a slice of pizza on a paper plate and handed it to Grandpa. "Oh, shucks. I forgot drinks."

"I didn't." He grinned. "Be right back."

"The Silver Fox thinks of everything." Max winked.

Grandpa came back from the kitchen with two cold bottles of diet soda.

"And what if I hadn't forgotten drinks?" I asked.

"Then you'd have had these here whenever you needed them."

I smiled. "You really do think of everything, don't you?"

"Don't give her credit for that," Max said. "I said it first."

As we ate, I told Grandpa all about the wedding party who'd come in today. "It's a terrific start for my business—a wedding right off the bat."

Max had patiently listened to my telling Grandpa about the bridesmaids' gowns I'd designed and that the women had been so happy with, but now she was champing at the bit to talk about Mark Tinsley.

"Dave, how can Amanda and I find out who killed the web designer?" she asked. "Our main suspects are Connie, Janice, and Ford."

"I don't know that—"

"Frank and Ella could have done it," Max interrupted my protest, "because Mark did such a lousy job on their website, or Mrs. Mecham could've whacked him for not paying his rent, but we don't think those are strong enough motives. Frank and Ella could've simply refused to pay until Mark did a more satisfactory job, and Mrs. Meacham had already found someone to take over Mark's space."

"All right," Grandpa said. "Tell me why you suspect the other three."

Max floated off the desk and paced the room. "Connie behaved strangely when Amanda saw her at the restaurant with Guy. Who's to say Connie and Guy aren't in cahoots on something—maybe blackmailing Janice? Mark found out and tried to protect his lady love and was rewarded with a bullet to the chest."

She gauged Grandpa's expression before continuing.

"If you don't buy that bag of apples, how about this: Maybe Mark discovered whatever it is Ford hides in his hollowed-out books. I mean, he could be putting anything in there—drugs, stolen money, hooch, blackmail materials."

"Blackmail must've been a big deal in your day," I said.

"Darling, blackmail is a big deal every day."

"What's this about Ford hollowing out books?" Grandpa asked.

"Max has witnessed Ford carving out hiding places in some of his books."

"That's odd," he said. "But, continue, Max. Why is Janice a suspect?"

"Because of the love affair, of course. Maybe she was through with Mark and didn't want to have to look at him every day."

"But she wouldn't have had to look at him every day," I pointed out. "Mark was leaving at the end of the month."

"Well, there is that...but she might've forgotten it." She planted her hands on her hips. "Passionate people aren't always the most logical."

"That's true." Grandpa wiped his mouth with his napkin. "But what if Mark was the one who was through with Janice?"

She wagged her index finger. "The wronged woman. I like it. Of course, his mother knew about Janice, so that would lead me to think she was more than a fling...to him, anyway." She resumed her pacing. "We know so little about Mark's personal life and why he was unable—or unwilling—to pay his rent. Amanda, you need to speak with Ms. Tinsley and see what you can dig up."

"Me? Why me?"

"Well, I can't very well do it, can I?"

I huffed. "I barely know the woman, and I don't have her phone number."

"I imagine Connie does. After all, it was she who hosted the séance."

I turned to Grandpa. "What do you think? Should I call Mark's grieving mother?"

He inclined his head, and I knew him well enough to know he was trying to reach a conclusion that would placate both Max and me. "It probably wouldn't hurt to call Ms. Tinsley and see how the poor woman is doing. You don't have to interrogate her, but you could let her know the people at Shops on Main haven't forgotten her or her son." He glanced at Max. "And if Ms. Tinsley feels the need to share anything more, then she'll have her opportunity."

"All right. I'll get the number from Connie tomorrow morning."

Max ran her hand along her throat. "I wonder how we can get a gander at Ford's and Janice's stuff." She pierced Grandpa with a stare. "How are you at lock-picking, Dave?"

"Not good. Plus, that's unethical."

She scoffed. "You and your granddaughter are wet blankets."

"You go into their shops all the time," I reminded Max. "Why do you suddenly want to pick their locks?"

"I'm unable to open drawers and go through files and things."

"No, but you can look through their electronic devices like phones, tablets, laptops and computers."

"Amanda! That's as bad—if not more so—than breaking into these people' offices," Grandpa Dave chided. "What happened to innocent until proven guilty?"

"How are we going to know whether they're innocent or guilty unless we go through their stuff?" Max asked.

"The way the old-fashioned detectives did—by asking questions."

Before we could debate the matter further, we heard the front door open. I froze, wide-eyed.

Gayle Leeson

"I thought you locked the door," Grandpa whispered.

"I did."

The person who'd opened the door apparently stood in the hallway for a moment, and then the floor creaked as he began to walk.

"What if it's Mark's killer?" I asked. "What if—"

"Hold your horses." Max went over and poked her head through the wall. She looked back around at Grandpa and me. "Relax. It's the Meacham kid."

I blew out a breath, put down my plate, and walked over to the door. I opened it just as Brett was reaching for the doorknob on the other side.

"Hi, Brett. Come on inside and meet my grandpa."

Brett shoved his hands into the pockets of his jeans and strode into the room. "I'm sorry to bother you folks, but I saw the light on as I was driving by, and I was concerned. I wanted to stop and make sure everything was all right."

"Mrs. Meacham certainly has an asset in you," Grandpa said, putting down his plate and reaching out his hand. "I'm Dave Tucker. Nice to meet you."

Brett shook his hand. "Brett Meacham. Nice to meet you, sir."

"Would you like to have some pizza?" I asked.

Grandpa laughed. "I sometimes have to make Amanda take a dinner break."

"Mom says the same thing about me," Brett said. "But, no, thank you. I won't take up anymore of your time. Just…you know…with all the stuff that's been going on, I wanted to make sure everything was okay." He lowered his eyes. "I couldn't forgive myself if someone else…well, you know."

"Thank you for checking on us," I said.

He smiled. "Anytime. I…uh…I hope to see you again soon."

After Brett had left, Max turned to me with a wicked grin. "It seems someone has a crush on our Amanda."

I could feel my cheeks burning. "I don't think so. He was right to be concerned that there were people in the building this late."

"Yeah, yeah." She waggled her eyebrows at Grandpa, and he laughed.

"I suppose we should be finishing up and calling it a night," he said.

After I got home, took my bath, and slipped into my pjs, I bit the bullet and called my parents. I hadn't planned to, but Grandpa Dave had spoken with me about it when we walked out of Shops on Main together.

"Have you spoken with your mom and dad since you opened Designs on You?" he'd asked.

"No." I avoided meeting his eyes. "Have you?"

"Yes, but I haven't told them about your new venture. I feel that's up to you."

So, I'd promised to call them. I half-hoped they'd be out, so I could leave a friendly message on their answering machine: *Hi! Just calling to say I love you, I hope all is well, and I've opened my own fashion design shop! Talk soon!*

No such luck. Mom answered on the third ring.

"Mandy, are you okay?"

"I'm fine, Mom. How are you?"

"I'm all right. Are you sure everything is all right? You call so seldom…"

"Yes. I'm…I had dinner with Grandpa Dave this evening."

"Well, thank goodness for him. At least, someone is around to keep an eye on you and make sure you aren't getting yourself into too much trouble."

I didn't remind her that I was almost twenty-five and hadn't done any jail time yet. I did, however, take a deep breath and tell her that I'd opened Designs on You.

"You've done what?"

"I've opened a fashion design shop called Designs on You," I repeated.

"Amanda Michelle Tucker, have you lost your mind? After all the money spent for your education, and you go and blow it on some hare-brained scheme like this?"

I could've said that Grandpa Dave spent the money for my education and that he supported my new venture, but I kept my mouth shut.

"How'd you get the money to set up a fashion boutique, of all things?" Mom ranted. "Let me guess— Grandpa Dave. When are you going to stop taking advantage of that man?"

"I'm not taking advantage of him. I'm paying him back for—"

"What in the world were you thinking?"

I wanted to speak with Dad. He was like Grandpa Dave…not as…judgmental. But I didn't dare ask. Maybe if she didn't get the responses she wanted, she'd hand me over to him anyway. She did.

"David, come speak with your daughter. You aren't going to believe what she's done now!"

"Hi, sweetheart."

"Hi, Dad."

"I understand you've lost your mind."

"Apparently so." I explained to him what I'd done. He didn't interrupt, so I was able to tell him about the shop, the loan from Grandpa Dave, and the gowns I'd received commissions for today.

"That's wonderful." He raised his voice. "And you didn't think to consult your mom or me before diving into this thing?" Lowered it again. "I'm proud of you."

I giggled. "Thanks, Dad."

"Your mom is too. She'll come around in a day or two and give you a call back."

"All right."

"I'll work on her," he promised.

"I love you."

"Oh, I know. I'm absolutely your favorite."

I laughed again. "Goodnight, Dad."

Raised voice, "Of course, you didn't! That's your problem, Amanda!" Lowered voice, "Goodnight. I love you."

I called Grandpa Dave as soon as I ended the call to my parents. "I told them."

"I thought I heard shouting from the general direction of Florida." He chuckled. "Seriously, how did it go?"

"About as well as could be expected. Mom thinks I've lost my mind, and Dad pretended to go along with her but said he's proud of me."

"Did you mention Mark Tinsley?"

"No. I thought it was best not to mention the murder or the ghost. If Mom thought I'd lost my mind simply because I'd set up shop, she'd have me committed if I told her my new best friend is a ghost."

"Ain't that the truth? I agree that it's best you don't ever mention Max…at least, not to your mother. And tell them about Mark only when his murder is solved."

"You don't think they might've read about the murder online and simply didn't connect it to the place where I've opened Designs on You, do you?" I asked.

"I doubt it. If your dad had seen anything about it, he'd have likely mentioned it to me. He doesn't keep up with Abingdon as much as he did when he and your mother first moved to Florida."

"I realize I should talk with them more, Grandpa Dave, but they just don't get me the way you do. And Max and Jason are the first friends I've had since graduating college."

"That happens, Pup. High school, college, workplaces…you always have the best intentions to keep up with the people you've befriended, but you seldom do."

"So, you don't think I've lost my mind?"

"Oh, I didn't say that. As Lewis Carroll said in Alice's Adventures in Wonderland, 'You're entirely bonkers…but..the best people are.'"

Chapter Seventeen

I arrived at Designs on You and let Jazzy out of her crate. After making sure she was settled in and had fresh kibble, I went over to talk with Connie.

"Hey, there! How are you?" Connie was as bubbly as ever in a blue and white tie-dyed tunic, leggings, and sandals. "I saw what appeared to be a bridal party entering your shop yesterday morning."

"That was indeed a bridal party, and I've been commissioned to do the bridesmaids' dresses."

She gave me a high five. "Congratulations!"

"Thank you." I thought about how much I'd liked Connie before that whole weirdness at the restaurant and Guy. I hoped I'd regain that feeling soon.

I looked around Delightful Home. Connie had replaced the curtains with green-and-white gingham.

"I like the new curtains," I said. "Very pretty."

She smiled. "I appreciate that. I feel it's a major compliment coming from you. I finished them last night and came in early this morning to hang them."

"I didn't realize you were a fellow seamstress."

Gayle Leeson

"Hardly," Connie said. "I can make a simple skirt, sew a pillow, and whip up some curtains, but I wouldn't even try to do what you do."

I browsed Connie's shelves of essential oils and selected a bottle of lavender. "I love lavender oil in my bath, and I'm just about out."

"These oils are excellent quality...wildcrafted and organic. I think you'll love it. And, of course, if you don't, I have a money-back guarantee."

As I paid for my purchase, I asked Connie if she had Lorinda Tinsley's phone number. At Connie's raised brows, I explained, "I'd like to call and see how she's doing. I realize I didn't know Mark, but I want Ms. Tinsley to feel that the people at Shops on Main care about her...and her son."

Connie stepped around the counter to give me a hug. "Aren't you the sweetest?" She took out her phone, copied Lorinda Tinsley's number from her contacts and texted it to me.

"I saw Guy come in with flowers," I said. "Are he and Janice working things out?"

"He told me yesterday that he's cautiously optimistic."

"That's good." I held up my Delightful Home bag. "Thank you!"

"Thank you. I'll talk with you later."

I opened the door into the reception area of Designs on You to see Max dancing for Jazzy. The cat was following

Max around and would occasionally flop down and roll onto her back while gazing up at the ghostly fashionista.

"What have you been doing while I've been entertaining the troops?" Max asked.

"I've been visiting with Connie." I walked through to the atelier.

"What did you buy?"

"Lavender essential oil. It's so relaxing in a bath." I opened the filing cabinet and placed the small bag in the back.

"You don't have to do that," Max said. "It won't bother me. In fact, I quite like the scent of lavender."

"It's not you I'm concerned about. Lavender oil can be toxic to cats."

"Well, you learn something new every day." She looked down at Jazzy, who'd followed us. "You're much loved, little Jazzy cat. We don't want you getting sick off lavender oil."

I got a cup of coffee, returned to the reception area, and took out my phone. I motioned for Max to join me as I placed my phone on the round table between the two chairs.

She clasped her hands as she hovered above the chair across from mine. "You got Mark's mother's telephone number, didn't you?"

"I did. But I'm a little hesitant to call from here. I'm afraid the walls have ears in this place."

Max scoffed. "Only when I'm around. And who can I tell except you? Besides, if you don't call from here, I'll miss out on the conversation, and two minds are always better than one when you're trying to sort things out."

"Agreed. Still, let's give everyone a few minutes to get settled in before we call. We don't want to be interrupted."

"Nor do we want to be too busy to talk with Mr. Handsome should he come down first thing to ask a certain someone for a date this weekend," Max said. "I'm telling you, you should invite the man to dinner."

"I might. I—" Before I could finish my thought, Max was gone.

In a few seconds, she was back. "Connie is scrolling through her phone. Frank and Ella are discussing their niece. Mrs. Meacham isn't here yet. Ford is playing solitaire on his desktop. And Jason is setting up for his first appointment." She nodded at the phone. "Dial."

I took a sip of my coffee, took a deep breath, and called Ms. Tinsley. The woman answered on the first ring.

"Yes? Hello?"

"Good morning, Ms. Tinsley. It's Amanda Tucker from Shops on Main. I hope I didn't wake you."

"No...you didn't. I barely sleep at all these days."

"I'm sorry. I can't imagine what you must be going through," I said.

"I miss him so much. He moved back in with me a few months ago. I believe he could see how lonely I was. He was a kind young man...giving up his apartment for me...He was special."

"I'm sure. Was Mark your only child, Ms. Tinsley?"

"Yes. Walter—Mark's father—and I divorced when Mark was just four years old. I never remarried. I was too afraid Mark would feel as if he were second best or that another man wouldn't love him like his own child." She took a shuddering breath. "I saw how Mark's stepmother treated him. "That woman only loved the child she brought into the marriage with Walter. She largely ignored Mark."

"That's terrible."

"Isn't it? And yet, Mark still adored his father. It would've broken his heart to know that Walter didn't even attend the funeral." Her voice cracked, and she was silent for a moment. I could well imagine she was composing herself before speaking again. "I couldn't even locate Walter to tell him about Mark's death."

"I'm so, so sorry," I said. "Everyone at Shops on Main misses Mark. I wish I could've known him longer."

"I wish so too. I'm sure you would've been great friends."

"We're here for you, Ms. Tinsley, if you need to talk." The words were hollow, I knew, but I meant them. I'd be

Gayle Leeson

happy to talk with this poor woman if it would help her in the least.

After ending the call, I looked at Max. "I feel like a hypocrite. I didn't go to Mark's funeral, and I only met the man once. And here I am calling his mother like he and I were great friends."

"You didn't tell her the two of you were great friends. You're only a hypocrite if you misrepresent yourself." She raised and dropped one shoulder. "Besides, you made Lorinda Tinsley feel better. That's a good thing. She's devastated and so horribly alone."

"I know. How horrible that Mark's dad missed the funeral."

"Given the way Ms. Tinsley talked, he might not have known about it. It doesn't appear she went to any extremes to find him."

"I wonder if maybe Mark and his father had drifted apart," I said.

"I don't think so. I heard Mark talking on the phone to his dad quite often. And he'd always tell the man to be careful and to take care of himself."

"Huh. That makes me wonder if Walter Tinsley is sick. Or was sick. Maybe the reason Ms. Tinsley couldn't find him was because he was dead."

I moved over to the desk and opened my laptop. A search for Walter Tinsley's obituary didn't turn up the person I'd expected, but it did give me another clue as to the man's whereabouts.

"Look," I told Max, then realized she was already there reading over my shoulder.

I'd found an obituary for Elizabeth Tinsley, which said she was survived by her spouse Walter of Allendale Village, beloved son Cole and wife Mara of Chattanooga, Tennessee, and stepson Mark of Abingdon, Virginia.

"Beloved son Cole," Max sneered. "It's obvious Lorinda Tinsley didn't make up that bit about the stepmom's favoritism."

I'd already opened another tab and was looking up Allendale Village. It was an assisted living facility.

"Call them," Max urged.

"And say what? Should I ask to talk with Walter Tinsley?"

"Yes."

"Do you want me to tell the man his son is dead?" I asked, shaking my head.

"No, of course not! Just...I don't know...ask him how's tricks."

I was gaping at her slack-jawed when my door opened. I quickly closed my mouth and greeted my customer.

Just before lunchtime, Connie popped in to ask if I'd spoken with Ms. Tinsley.

"I did. What do you know about Mark's father?"

"I don't know anything about him...but Janice might."

I inclined my head. "I hesitate to ask Janice because I'm afraid she'll think I'm only being nosy, but I'm actually concerned." I explained to Connie how I'd found the obituary for Mark's stepmother and learned that his father is—or was at that time—in an assisted living facility.

"How long ago was that?" Connie asked.

"About six months ago. Ms. Tinsley said she'd tried to contact Mark's father to let him know about Mark's death, but she couldn't find him."

"And did you call her back to tell her you'd located him?"

"I didn't," I said. "I was afraid that maybe he'd...moved on...or something."

"You didn't call the facility to ask if he was there." It was a flat statement rather than a question. "I'll speak with Janice and see what she knows."

Once she'd left, I quickly went to the kitchen and took my chicken salad sandwich from the refrigerator. I hadn't seen Max since the customer came in after I'd spoken with Ms. Tinsley. The customer had wanted "something similar" to the dress on the mannequin. I'd showed her some pattern books, and we'd spoken at length on how I might modify the design to better suit her. Then she'd left with the promise that she might be back.

Now I was struggling to get my bridesmaids' muslins finished. My plan was to wolf down my sandwich and get back to work.

Really. That was the plan.

But then I heard Jason speak to Frank as was he was walking up the stairs, so I decided to give him a moment to get settled into his studio and then go invite him to dinner tomorrow evening. Since Max hadn't been around for a while, I thought it was a great opportunity to speak with Jason alone.

All the way up the stairs, I looked over my shoulder. No sign of the sassy specter.

I stood in front of Jason's door willing my heart to stop racing before I tapped. I knocked so lightly, I was afraid he hadn't heard it. In fact, I'd decided that if he hadn't heard it, I'd go back to Designs on You and forget the whole thing.

The door opened, and there he stood. I felt as if my heart was dropping to the floor.

"Hi." He smiled. "This is a nice surprise." He moved aside. "Come on in."

I walked into the studio, and the first thing I saw was Max. She was sitting on a stool in front of a bucolic backdrop with her head thrown back and one leg extended into the air.

"Take my photograph!" she shouted.

Jason followed my gaze and must've noticed my expression of dismay. "Is something wrong?"

"I just...it looks as if you're getting ready for a client. I don't want to intrude on your preparations."

"We're good. That was for the client who was here before lunch."

"Oh..." I let out a breath. "I—"

The camera clicked, and the flash sent a burst of light into the room.

I held up both hands. "It wasn't me. I didn't touch anything."

"I'm sure you didn't." Jason grinned. "That was strange, though, wasn't it?" He went over to the camera and looked at the screen. "Check this out."

I was afraid to look at what the camera had captured, but it would be weird if I feigned disinterest. I took a step closer to the camera and saw a photo of the serene backdrop with a blurry streak across the center.

"Rats! I moved!" Max huffed. "Let's try another."

"No," I hissed.

Jason arched an eyebrow.

"No, way!" I said. "That really is odd. Do you think I bumped it…or?"

"You couldn't have. You weren't close enough." He winked. "All these historic buildings have ghosts, you know."

I forced out a laugh and turned to go, but then I mustered up my courage again. "Jason, I'm making lasagna for dinner tomorrow evening. Would you care to join me?"

"I'd like that very much."

Max let out a squeal of delight. "This is fantastic! Still, I wish I could've gotten a do-over on my photograph. Work on making that happen, would you?"

I was so focused on the muslin I was cutting out that I started when Connie opened the door to the atelier.

"I'm sorry. I didn't cause you to mess anything up, did I?" she asked.

I shook my head.

"Good." She came on inside and shut the door. "I spoke with Janice. Mark's dad has Parkinson's disease.

After Mark's stepmom died in a car accident last year, Walter couldn't take care of himself and had to go into assisted living. The treatment and the facility costs quickly drained his bank accounts."

"Oh, no." I raised my hand to my lips.

"He couldn't even sell the house because it had been in his wife's name, and she left everything she had to her son Cole. Walter got nothing."

"That's why Mark couldn't pay his rent here anymore," I said. "Or the rent on his apartment. Everything he made was going to pay his father's bills."

"And it still wasn't enough. The assisted living facility is kicking Walter out at the end of this month."

"What's he going to do?"

"Janice didn't say," Connie said. "It's probable that she doesn't know. But it's a horrible situation."

I wholeheartedly agreed with her there. After Connie left, I got my phone and made another call to Ms. Tinsley.

"Ms. Tinsley, I realize this isn't my place, but I was able to track down Mark's father." I told her what I'd learned.

"Poor, poor Walter," Ms. Tinsley said softly. "He doesn't even know Mark is dead. I have to go and tell him. Thank you, dear."

I hoped I'd sent her on a mission of mercy, not one that would merely lead to more pain for them both.

Designs On Murder

Chapter Eighteen

I was determined to get at least one of the bridesmaid's muslins done before quitting for the day. It was past closing time, and most of the vendors at Shops on Main had left, but I was so close to finishing that I wasn't going to stop.

The front door opened, and I heard someone in the hall. The footsteps stopped outside Designs on You, and my shoulders slumped. I didn't want to wait on a customer. I wanted to sew up this pattern.

"Be right there!" I called, when my visitor stepped into the reception area.

"How about I come to you?"

I let out my breath in a relieved whoosh. It was Grandpa Dave. He walked into the atelier with a folded newspaper tucked beneath his left arm.

"Hello, Dave."

He quickly turned to see Max standing directly behind him. "Oh, hi, Max. I didn't realize you were here."

"I wasn't. I was upstairs trying to do some reconnaissance when my heart started thumping a mile a minute. That's how I knew you were here." She batted her eyes.

"Is that true?" I asked. "Does your heart still beat?"

"Of course not, darling. I was speaking figuratively."

"How is your recon going?" Grandpa asked her.

"Not well, I'm afraid."

Grandpa took the paper from beneath his arm and unfolded it on the worktable. "I probably shouldn't be stirring the pot like this, but the jewelry you two discovered in Janice's shop didn't look anything like this…did it?"

I got up from behind the sewing machine to step closer to the worktable. The newspaper's grainy photo showed a beautiful pair of dress clips and an ornately-carved emerald cabochon and diamond ring.

Shaking my head, I said, "No. I've never seen these before."

"Good," Grandpa said, "because they're stolen."

"I've seen them," Max said. "They're upstairs in Janice's shop."

"That's a serious accusation," I said. "Are you sure?"

"Positive. I'm not saying Janice stole anything, but if those aren't the pieces Janice has upstairs in the pouch with the Tiffany bracelet, then they're exact replicas." She nodded at Grandpa. "Call in the coppers, Dave."

Before Grandpa could respond, I said, "We can't report this to the police! What would we say? Our friend the ghost says the stolen jewelry you're looking for is upstairs?"

"I wouldn't say *ghost*," Max said. "That stretches the bounds of credibility."

I sighed and looked up at the ceiling.

Grandpa asked if I saw either of the items from the newspaper while I was looking at the Tiffany bracelet.

"No. I mean, I could tell there were other items in the pouch," I said, "but I was all about that bracelet."

"What if we alert Mrs. Meacham to the fact that there could be stolen property in Janice's shop?" Max waved a hand. "She has a key—she could go in and take a look."

"A landlord isn't permitted inside a tenant's shop without advance written notice except in cases of emergency," Grandpa said.

Max huffed. "Doesn't this constitute an emergency?"

He shook his head. "The types of emergency covered by the law include flooding…fire…things like that."

"Got a match?"

"Max!" I exclaimed.

"Oh, pipe down. I'm only kidding." She paced around the room. "However, if I could trigger that ceiling device…"

"Ceiling device?" I looked up at my own ceiling. There in the corner was a smoke detector. "You mean, the smoke alarm?"

"Maybe." She shrugged. "Once Janice smoked a gasper in there, and the thing made an outrageous racket."

"That's a good idea," Grandpa said. "Max could set off the smoke detector—"

"Wait," I interrupted. "How?"

"The same way I made the camera take my photograph." She pushed out her bottom lip. "I still wish I could've gotten a do over."

"If we can somehow pull this off, I promise I'll try to take your photograph," I said.

She clapped enthusiastically. "Yay!"

Grandpa smiled at her. "You're a treasure." He looked back at me. "Both of you, I mean."

"Yeah, right." I shook my head. My grandpa was smitten with a ghost. How weird was that? "Now whatever we're going to do, we need to do it quickly before Mrs. Meacham leaves."

"Nah, we still have some time," Max said. "Mrs. Meacham often stays late to read or to watch a movie or something on her laptop before going home. She's reading now. I heard her tell someone over the phone once that she takes full advantage of her time before the caretaker leaves, especially before the weekend."

"That's sad that she doesn't want to go home." Poor Mrs. Meacham. George was sweet, but I imagined it would be burdensome to take care of him.

"But that's advantageous to us," Grandpa said. "So, Max, if you can find a way to sound the smoke alarm, Amanda and I will follow Mrs. Meacham into Janice's shop to see how we can help. Amanda can slip the pouch out of the drawer, and I'll hide it inside this folded newspaper."

I shook my head. "It's too risky! What if Mrs. Meacham catches us?"

He picked up the newspaper, refolded it, and placed it under his arm. "We could simply show her this article and tell her the truth—that we think Janice is in possession of the stolen jewelry."

"And if the jewelry isn't in the pouch?" I asked.

He blew out a breath. "I don't know, Pup."

"Furthermore, how will we return the pouch to Janice's shop?"

"She has a point," Max said. "We don't want that guy—Guy—coming after us...well, coming after the two of you."

"We'll play the whole thing by ear," Grandpa said. "It's our only chance. If Janice—or whomever stole the jewelry—sees this article, they're going to move it."

"All right." I turned to Max. "It's still in the same place?"

She nodded and was gone.

Grandpa and I went through the reception area to wait at the bottom of the stairs. Connie, Frank, and Ella had left already, so we had the downstairs to ourselves. No one was around to ask why we were standing by the stairs…you know, as if we were waiting for a smoke alarm to go off so we could dash up and steal some already-stolen jewelry.

When the smoke alarm's shrill beep sounded, I started to sprint up the stairs immediately. Grandpa took my arm, shook his head, and counted to three. Then we hurried up the stairs to find Mrs. Meacham already standing outside Janice's door.

"If that woman has left a candle burning," Mrs. Meacham said, "so help me, I'm tossing her out. I've warned her about that."

She unlocked the door, and Grandpa and I followed her inside.

"I don't see any smoke," Grandpa said.

I hurried to the round table in the center of the room. "Neither do I."

Mrs. Meacham stepped out into the hall where she retrieved a step ladder from a closet. She brought the ladder back into the shop, climbed up, and turned off the smoke detector. I eased the drawer open, removed the pouch, and put it behind my back.

I felt Grandpa take it from me.

As Mrs. Meacham started to step off the ladder, the alarm sounded again. "What, the--?" She stepped up again, took down the device, and stared at the battery.

"Maybe it needs a new battery. I'll be right back. Would you two mind looking around to see if you can find anything amiss?"

"Not at all," Grandpa said.

Mrs. Meacham went back out to the closet where the ladder had been stored. Apparently, she didn't find any batteries there, so she went downstairs.

"Hurry!" I hissed, taking my phone from my pocket.

Grandpa dumped the pouch out onto the table. Sure enough, there were the dress clips and the ring that were in the newspaper. The Tiffany bracelet was there too, as were another bracelet and a brooch. I opened the camera app and quickly snapped photos of the jewelry. I was even able to get the manufacturer's information in some of the pictures before I heard Mrs. Meacham's footsteps on the stairs.

As I put away my phone, Grandpa shoved everything into the pouch and put it back into the drawer. By the time Mrs. Meacham reentered the shop, he and I were looking around at everything as if we were searching for a fire. Max was standing by the door blowing on her fingernails and looking way too pleased with herself. I could only hope I didn't look as much like a maniac as I felt. If I did, Mrs. Meacham would see right through me.

But the efficient woman didn't say a word. She simply climbed the ladder and returned the smoke detector to its proper place, now with a fresh battery intact.

"Let me put that away for you," Grandpa said, folding the ladder once Mrs. Meacham had completed her task.

"I'd appreciate that, Mr. Tucker."

Grandpa was reminding her to call him Dave when the three of us stepped out of Janice's shop.

My mouth went dry as I saw Ford leaning against the doorjamb of his shop, arms folded, eyes narrowed. Unable to speak, I merely stared at him.

"Move your feet," Max whispered in my left ear. "Do it. Calmly walk down the stairs."

And somehow, I did.

When we got back to Designs on You and were in the atelier with the door shut, I ran both hands through my hair.

"Ford was watching us," I wailed. "He knows what we did."

"So what?" Grandpa asked. "He might've seen us taking photographs of jewelry in Janice's shop, but we can say…" He stumbled over that one for a moment. "We can say it was for insurance purposes. That's it. We were photographing some of the pieces in case there was something to be concerned about because the smoke detector kept going off inexplicably."

I pulled out one of my sewing machine chairs, sank onto it, and put my head between my knees.

"Deep breaths...I think," Max said. "Just do whatever you need to do to keep from fainting."

"She's right, Amanda. You need to pull yourself together and show us those photographs."

"Get her a glass of water, Dave."

Grandpa followed Max's instructions and went to the kitchen for a glass of water.

I sat up and drank it. It helped.

"Feeling better?" he asked.

I nodded. "What about Ford?"

Max waved her arms. "Never mind Ford. He has secrets of his own. He cuts the middles out of books, remember?"

I gasped. "That's right. What if it's to transport stolen jewelry? What if he and Janice are partners?"

"Nah," Max said. "The pillowcase and the book vendor aren't on swell terms. They seldom speak and that's only when they're passing each other in the hallway or something."

"But that could be their cover," I said.

"They don't need a cover when they believe they're the only people here," she said.

"Come on." Grandpa waggled two fingers. "Get your phone out so we can look at those photos."

I scooted the chair over and put the phone on the worktable. As I pulled up the photo gallery, Grandpa moved to look over my shoulder and Max came around the other side.

The first one was of an emerald and diamond Art Deco bangle with black stones which could've been jet or onyx. It was a gorgeous piece, but even after enlarging the photo, I couldn't see a maker's mark. Max said she believed it was Van Cleef & Arpels.

Photo number two was a closeup of an intricately carved emerald and diamond ring. Had I not read the description of the ring in the newspaper, I'd have thought the carved stone was jade rather than emerald. That only served to show that I didn't know much about jewelry. The article had proclaimed the ring to be a J.E. Caldwell & Co. ring worth over twenty-two thousand dollars.

In the same photo with the ring was the Tiffany bracelet. Again, I could see no manufacturer's mark or serial number or anything, but I recognized—and still loved—the piece.

The next photograph showed the Cartier dress clips. They, too, were identifiable from the photo in the newspaper, and one was open so we could see the manufacturer's name on the inside. Also in this photo was a brooch that was face down upon the table, and when we enlarged the photo, we could see *BVCCELLATI* inscribed on the clasp.

"Buccellati," Max breathed.

"Who's that?" Grandpa asked.

"An Italian jewelry designer. Aunt June discovered his boutique in Milan in 1922."

"We have what we need." Grandpa fished his phone out of his pocket. "I'm calling the police."

Max and I listened while he called the police department. He asked for the officer whose name was given in the newspaper as the person in charge of the investigation. The officer was off duty, but the dispatcher said she'd call him immediately.

Grandpa took a seat at the worktable while I got up and paced. It seemed like forever, although it couldn't have been more than five minutes, until his phone rang.

He answered. "Yes, this is Dave Tucker." He explained that we'd taken photos of some jewelry that we believed to be the stolen items in question. The officer asked for our location, and Grandpa told him. When Grandpa placed his phone into his pocket, he said, "Officer Cranston is on his way."

Officer Cranston looked to be in his early forties, had sandy hair, blue eyes, and a serious expression on his face. After introducing himself, he said, "Let's see what you've got."

I pulled up the images on my phone and handed them to the officer.

"Where did you take these?" Officer Cranston asked.

"Upstairs at Janice's Jewelry," I said. "We had our suspicions after I found a bracelet there the other day. This evening when the smoke alarm went off, we went inside and while Mrs. Meacham went for a battery, we took these to see if the pieces were the same as the ones in the paper."

"Why didn't you alert the landlord? Do you believe she's culpable?"

"No, sir, I don't." I bit my lip. "I was worried I'd be wrong and look like a fool."

"All right. Would you open your email account please? I want to email your photographs to myself."

I did as he asked, and he took my phone, entered his email address, and sent himself the photographs. Then he deleted the photos from my phone.

"You don't need those images on your phone," he said. "Too incriminating should someone else see them. I'm going to use them to get a search warrant. In the meantime, I want you folks to go on home."

"All right." Grandpa Dave shook the officer's hand. "Thank you, sir."

"W-will Janice know…this was…us?" I asked, as I put Jazzy into her carrier.

Officer Cranston shook his head. "We'll say only that we received an anonymous tip. Mr. Tucker, we have your cell phone number from where you called the station. I'll let you know when we have the suspect in custody if it will ease your minds."

"Yes. Please do that," Grandpa said.

I turned to look back at Max as Grandpa ushered me out the door. "Goodnight."

She waved.

The officer said, "Goodnight. Don't worry. Everything will be fine."

Grandpa Dave went home with me and Jazzy to await Officer Cranston's call. That man had been wrong when he'd said everything would be fine. Everything was not fine. He got the search warrant, his officers went over every inch of Janice's shop, and they found nothing. Not. A. Single. Piece. Of. Stolen. Jewelry.

Chapter Nineteen

After Grandpa left, I got ready for bed even though I knew sleep would elude me. I felt as if I'd lost my balance and was about to fall...unsettled, ready to reach out and grasp at a safety net that wasn't there. Even though I realized it was illogical, I worried that Ford or Guy had followed me home and was waiting outside to come in and shoot me the way Mark Tinsley had been shot. Was this how it had happened to Mark? Had he discovered the stolen jewelry and confronted Janice? Had she then shot him? Or had Guy—her other boyfriend and partner in crime—killed him? Or what about Ford? Did he hollow out books so that he and Janice could transport the stolen jewelry in them undetected?

Someone had to have called Janice before the police returned with the search warrant and warned her that the stolen jewelry was about to be seized. That's what made me believe Ford might be Janice's partner. He'd been there when Grandpa and I had taken the photos. Grandpa had tried to assure me that maybe Ford hadn't seen anything, that he'd only been aware that we'd gone inside the shop with Mrs. Meacham to make sure everything was all right. But the fact remained that Officer Cranston's team hadn't found any stolen jewelry in the shop. And I couldn't imagine Mrs. Meacham would've been the one to alert Janice…unless the landlord had called her tenant as a courtesy to tell her what had happened.

I heard a noise outside and a scream escaped my throat before I realized I was making a sound. I wanted to see what it was, but I was afraid to go to the windows. Finally, not knowing was too unbearable, and I went to peep out the side of the living room window. The neighbor's dog was on the porch, tail wagging. Normally, I'd give the spotted hound a treat—I kept a box of dog biscuits for him—but not tonight. Tonight, I was too scared to open the door.

I finally went to bed, but I left a light on in the living room and one on in the hallway to make any would-be intruders think I was either not alone or awake and alert enough to call the police. I didn't get much sleep, but when I slept, I had fitful, disjointed nightmares: images of Ford with his arms folded as he glared at me; Janice's look of panic when she saw me trying on the Tiffany bracelet; Guy brusquely passing me on the stairs on his way up to Janice's shop; Sabine, the psychic, talking about secrets; and George Meacham telling me about riding the Birmingham Special to Bristol with his sticky-fingered little brother.

I was glad the next morning when Jazzy woke me with her sandpapery tongue on my forehead.

Rather than butterflies in my stomach, I felt as if I had a belly full of hatching chicks, all pecking and scratching and fluttering to escape their shells as I walked into Shops on Main. I was glad I didn't encounter anyone on my way into Designs on You and could quickly get inside and close the door behind me.

I was disappointed that Max wasn't inside waiting for me. I put down Jazzy's crate and let her out into the atelier. Then I said as loudly as I dared, "Max! Max, where are you! I need to see you now!"

My summons went unanswered, so I busied myself working on the bridesmaids' muslins. I'd been working for about forty-five minutes when the door between the atelier and the hall leading to the kitchen opened. I stopped sewing and faced the door.

"Good morning." Ford was smiling. From where I sat, the smile looked like the hungry snarl of a wolf. "I wanted to check on you after last night's excitement."

Gayle Leeson

"I'm fine," I said quickly. Then attempting to control my shaking voice, "Th-thank you."

"No problem. I hope you stay that way."

I raised my chin, determined not to cower before him. "What do you mean?"

"You need to be careful and think about things you're getting involved in. The next time a smoke detector goes off, it might not be a false alarm."

What did he mean? Was he threatening to set fire to my shop or something? I can't show weakness. I can't let him know how afraid I am.

"Even if it hadn't been a false alarm, I'd have wanted to be there to help Mrs. Meacham and Janice," I said. "Wouldn't you?"

"That depends on the level of risk. Had Mrs. Meacham opened the door to leaping flames, we'd have all been wise to evacuate the building. Don't you agree?"

"You'd have simply let your books burn?" I asked.

"Better to lose some books—or jewelry—than a life."

I nodded. "Of course."

"Just be careful." With that, he pulled the door closed.

I listened as he went into the kitchen and then, moments later, back down the hall. I still couldn't decide if he'd come to issue a warning or a threat.

When Max appeared a short time later, I demanded to know where she'd been.

"Didn't you hear me calling you this morning?"

Although Max was an ethereal being, I could've sworn her body stiffened and her face tightened. "I was under the impression that I was a friend, not a servant."

I closed my eyes, mortified at my behavior. "You are. I'm sorry, Max. I'm just freaking out." I explained to Max that Officer Cranston had phoned last night to let us know that the search of Janice's shop hadn't turned up the missing jewelry. "Apparently, Janice—or someone—took it and hid it elsewhere."

"Nothing? They found nothing?"

"Not a single piece…of stolen jewelry at least. Did you see Janice return or someone else go into her shop last night?"

"No," Max said. "It takes a lot of energy to be present here. I was gone as soon as you and Dave left. I didn't even try to watch the police search because I thought the case had been solved and that we were finished."

I apologized to Max again and stood. I held my arms out to hug her, and then I remembered I couldn't.

Gayle Leeson

She smiled sadly. "It's the thought that counts, chum."

"I'm scared," I admitted.

"I know. I'm frightened for you."

"You remember Ford standing there staring at us last night?"

Max nodded.

"He came in this morning to tell me to be careful and aware of the situations I get involved in."

"Who unlocked the shop to allow the police inside?" Max asked. "Was it Mrs. Meacham or Janice?"

"Officer Cranston didn't say. Why?"

"If it was Janice, she'd have had the opportunity to hide the jewels before they got here, so I don't think they'd have involved her. It must've been Mrs. Meacham."

"You don't think she's involved?"

"I can't imagine she would be. However, people can surprise you."

"Should I ask her who let the officers into the building?" I asked.

She shook her head. "Ask the officer, if you ask anyone. I have to agree with Ford on one thing—be careful. Don't trust anyone here until this case—especially Mark's murder—is solved."

Max watched *After The Thin Man* at the worktable while I sewed bridesmaids' muslins. When I had a customer, I'd pull the door up behind me and greet them in the reception area. By the end of the day, I was able to complete two more muslins. I felt confident I could finish the last one on Monday and get the women scheduled for their fittings. After that, the only delay would be waiting for the fabric to arrive, and it should be here within seven to ten days.

Near the end of the workday, I went upstairs to make sure Jason was still coming to dinner. When I knocked on the door of his studio, he said he'd just been coming down to see me.

My heart sank. He wasn't coming.

"What may I bring?" he asked.

I smiled, my heart soaring again. He was coming. "I don't need for you to bring anything."

"But I'd feel like a bum if I didn't bring something. How about dessert?"

"I never turn down dessert," I said.

After talking with Jason, I stepped back into the hallway to see Ford coming out of Antiquated Editions.

Gayle Leeson

"Do you have exciting plans for the weekend?" Ford asked, with a glance at Jason's door.

"Nothing too extravagant," I said. "How about you?"

"Extravagance isn't my forte either," he said.

I nodded toward Janice's door. "It appears Janice got a jump on all of us and started her weekend early."

"You think so?"

"That's how it looks," I said.

"Ah, but things are not always what they appear to be…are they?"

I bustled around the kitchen putting the finishing touches on the salad and checking the rolls I had in the oven while the lasagna was cooling on a trivet on the countertop. I half wished Max could be here to help me navigate this date. On the other hand, she'd undoubtedly wind up making me say something I'd regret.

I started to light the white taper candles Mom kept on the sideboard in case the power went out, but I was afraid that would make it appear that I was trying too hard. I also hoped Jason didn't read anything into the fact that our rolls were plain old yeast rolls rather than garlic bread.

No, I wasn't anticipating a goodnight kiss...not really...but I didn't want to have dragon breath either.

Being afraid Jason and I would find conversation awkward or stilted—or that I would anyway—I'd bought some conversation cards and placed them at the side of the table. There were questions such as *"what song did you hate when you were in your teens?"* and *"what was your favorite toy as a kid?"*

The doorbell rang, and I smoothed out the skirt of my pink, off-the-shoulder A-line dress. It was one I'd made from a late-1950s pattern. I wore flat sandals to make the look more casual.

I took my time walking to the door. I didn't want Jason to think I was nervous. Fine. I didn't want Jason to *know* I was nervous.

He was carrying a bakery bag and a bouquet of white lilies. "Hi, there. You look beautiful."

"Thank you." I bit my tongue just in time to avoid saying *so do you*. But he did. He wore jeans and a navy plaid button-down shirt that really brought out the color of his eyes. "Please come in."

Jason handed me the flowers as Jazzy wound around his ankles. "Oh, hey, Jazzy." He grimaced at me. "I'm sorry. I didn't think to bring anything for her."

"Trust me. She doesn't need anything, except maybe a chin scratch." I put the flowers on the island and retrieved a vase from under the sink.

The timer sounded to let me know the bread was done.

"If you'll point me in the direction of an oven mitt, I can get those out while you arrange your flowers," Jason said.

I handed him the oven mitts that were hanging on a peg to my right. As he took out the bread, he commented on how great everything smelled.

"I'm glad." I placed the flowers in the vase before filling it with water. "I hope the food tastes even better than it smells." I set the vase in the center of the table.

Jason moved the vase slightly after we'd taken our seats. "I hope you don't mind, but I want to be able to see you."

I laughed. "I don't mind at all." I nodded toward the bakery bag he'd left on the island. "What did you bring for dessert?"

He shook his head. "It's a surprise. Just don't eat so much of the main course that you don't have any room left."

"I'll try, but lasagna is a favorite."

"It's a favorite of mine too."

"What are your other favorite foods?" I asked.

"It would be less time consuming to ask what I don't like." He chuckled. "Lima beans…boiled cabbage…turnip soup."

"I've never tried turnip soup."

"Neither have I. It just sounds like something I wouldn't like."

I laughed.

We both filled our plates and were eating when Jason nodded toward the box of cards. "What's that?"

I felt a blush creep up my cheeks. "It was…they're…conversation cards. I was afraid we'd run out of things to talk about."

"Am I that boring?" he asked.

"I was afraid I was the one who'd be less than stellar company. I didn't sleep well last night."

"Why's that?"

I didn't dare tell him about the whole jewelry fiasco from the night before, not at this stage in our relationship. He might think I was a snoop or a gossip or a troublemaker. And, truthfully, I might be all of those things, but I felt like I merely wanted Mark Tinsley's killer brought to justice and to be able to feel safe at Shops on Main.

So I answered, "I'm anxious about getting Heather's bridesmaid dresses finished."

"When is the wedding?"

"In two months."

"Then don't you have plenty of time?"

I inclined my head. "Yes and no. I'll feel better when I get the muslins completed and the first fittings done. Then when the material arrives, I can sew up the dresses using the muslin patterns. It's all downhill after that. I'll call the women in for their second fittings and make any alterations." I sipped my soda. "I suppose the main thing is that these are the first bridesmaids' dresses I've ever done. I want Heather to be happy with them."

"I can identify." Jason went on to tell me about the first wedding he shot. "It's nerve-wracking. You want to do a fantastic job so that your client will recommend you to others, but you also want your client's special day to be as wonderful as he or she deserves it to be."

After dinner, Jason presented his desserts: single servings of tiramisu, turtle cheesecake, and chocolate cake, and one maple brownie.

My eyes widened. "You can't possibly mean for us to eat all of this?"

"Just a little taste of each."

"A little taste" turned into our eating most of all four desserts and being so miserable we could barely move. We went into the living room and slumped onto the sofa.

"I suppose a dance marathon is out of the question?" Jason asked.

"For a little while at least. This is as bad as Thanksgiving."

"No. This is as good as Thanksgiving." He slipped his hand into mine. "What really kept you from sleeping well last night? Was it bridesmaid dresses, or was it something else?"

I tried to keep my tone light. "Like what?"

"Like Mark Tinsley's murder."

"That does cross my mind regularly." I squeezed his hand. "How about you?"

"I wonder about it. It doesn't help that I'm in the space he occupied when...when he was shot to death."

"I know. That can't be easy. I just wish it was over, that whoever killed Mark was caught, and that all of us at Shops on Main could put this entire thing behind us."

"So do I...and with our being the new kids in town, we're at a disadvantage when it comes to guessing who the suspects might be," Jason said. "Don't you think? Or maybe you have someone in mind..."

I hesitated a moment too long.

"You have." He slowly grinned. "Who is it?"

How much should I tell him...if anything? Did I truly know Jason any better than I knew any of the other Shops on Main vendors?

"Come on," he cajoled.

"I...I think Ford is a little...shady," I said at last.

"Ford?" He scoffed. "Nah, he sells books. How sketchy could he be?"

"I don't know. I simply get the feeling he's hiding something. And Sabine did say that it was someone's secrets that got Mark killed."

"Aw, that was one of those vague things phony soothsayers spout to make you think they know what they're doing."

I didn't volunteer the information that Sabine hadn't seemed like a fake when she'd detected Max in my boutique. "All right then. Who do you think shot Mark?"

"In the detective shows, it's always the person you least suspect, right?"

I nodded.

"What do you know about Frank and Ella?" he asked.

Chapter Twenty

“Good morning, Pup!”

I was barely awake enough to answer the phone, and I blinked rapidly as I tried to clear my head. “Hi.”

“Did I wake you?”

“No, Grandpa. What’s up?”

“I’m sitting here looking at the newspaper, and there’s an estate sale that starts at two o’clock. I thought we could grab a bite of lunch and then head over. What do you say?”

“I think that’s a great idea.” I stifled a yawn. “What caught your eye?”

“They have some interesting furniture I believe I can refinish and resell.”

I smiled. Grandpa Dave would never be content to sit still for a minute. “Then we’re taking your truck?”

“Yep. I’ll pick you up around noon?”

“Sounds good.”

After ending the call, I raised up on my elbows and looked for Jazzy. She was curled up at the foot of the bed.

She wasn't sleeping, but she was looking at me contentedly.

"What's wrong with you?" I asked the little furball. "You'd normally wake me up way before now."

The cat raised her head, yawned, and nestled her face back between her paws.

"You have an excellent point." Still, I managed to resist the temptation to follow Miz Jasmine's lead and relax back under the covers. There were things I needed to do, like update the lookbook on my website and pay some bills. So, with one last longing look at my pillow, I got out of bed.

Jazzy sighed and then stood and stretched. She, too, seemed resigned to the fact that if I was getting out of bed, she might as well get up, eat, and then find another comfy spot to nap.

I fed the cat and then had a cup of coffee while I sketched a new design. The sketch was of an everyday jumpsuit—they were in fashion again—in a 1940s style. The jumpsuit I was creating had wide legs, a high waist, and three-quarter length sleeves. I'd create this one in denim, but I could adapt it to a variety of fabrics and colors.

As I was working on the jumpsuit's lines, the phone rang. I answered it without looking at the screen. I was guessing Grandpa thought of something else to tell me about the estate sale.

"Hello, Mandy."

Mom. I managed to hold back a sigh, but I did grit my teeth, expecting round two of the "I can't believe you did such an idiotic thing" battle.

"Good morning," I said stiffly. *Let's get this over with.*

"I'm sorry I was so quick to fly off the handle with you the other night," she said.

My jaw dropped. This wasn't like Mom. Was the woman dying? Did she think I was dying? *Was* I dying? Did she know something I didn't?

"Dave tells your Dad and me that you're doing well," Mom continued.

I let out a sigh of relief. Good old Grandpa Dave. He was behind this change of heart.

"Thank you. I believe things are going wonderfully." I told her about some of the commissions I'd gotten so far. I would have told her about Ruby and her frenemy—the groom's aunt—coming in on the first day, but Dad would appreciate that story more than Mom would, so I saved it for him.

"Your dad and I will see for ourselves in a few weeks."

"Oh...good." Was it good? I hoped it would be good. It could go either way. I mean, there was the question of the murder and the stolen jewelry and the fact that my business could all dry up in a few weeks... Or everything could be, well, good.

Also, there was Max. Would Mom and Dad be able to see Max like Grandpa could? Mom was saying something, so I tuned out my thoughts in order to concentrate on her voice.

"…fashion thing fails, you still have an excellent education to fall back on. And I suppose it's best you do this thing while you're young, so you have time to recover from a financial and career standpoint."

I gripped my pencil so tightly I was afraid it might break. Nothing like praise and encouragement from one's mommy. Still, at this stage of the game, it was as close to encouragement as I was likely to get from her. I thanked her and asked about Toffee, the Yorkshire terrier puppy she and Dad had adopted when they moved to Florida. I was happy to hear that Toffee was doing fine and that Mom had enough anecdotes about him to last for the rest of our conversation.

On the way to the restaurant, I told Grandpa about Mom's call.

"I owe you big time for telling them I was doing well," I said.

"You are doing well."

"Yeah, but…well, you know." I lolled my head against the back of the seat. "She's threatening to come for a visit in a few weeks."

"Don't borrow trouble, Pup. Cross that bridge when you get to it. All we're going to concern ourselves with today is what we can find at this estate sale."

"Right. And, by the way, I didn't mention anything about the stolen jewelry or the murder or Max or any of the really juicy stuff going on at Shops on Main."

"Neither did I."

"Oh, I could tell. Had you mentioned it, she and Dad would've been on their way up here to get me and drag me to Florida with them."

He chuckled. "Well, I'm not about to let that happen…at least, not if I can help it. I say we never say anything about any of the mysterious happenings unless we're either directly asked or wind up being celebrated heroes with our names in the news."

"Um, let's definitely keep our names out of the news. If they find out all of this was going on and we didn't tell them, they're going to be furious with both of us."

After a lunch of Parmesan chicken, wild rice, and green beans, Grandpa and I headed to the estate sale.

"I'm particularly interested in an Americana dining room set that was listed. If I can buy it and refinish it, I can probably make a nice profit from it."

Grandpa Dave pulled into a subdivision where a large ESTATE SALE sign let us know we were headed in the right direction. We drove past the immaculate two-story home where someone was obviously still caring for the lawn and exterior. I could only imagine the interior was as well-maintained. Since there were a number of vehicles already lining the street—and it was still about five minutes until two—we had to park two houses down and walk back.

The sellers hadn't let people in early, but they were opening the door just as we started up the walk. Ahead of us, I spotted Ford.

He turned, saw us, and fell back. "Hey, there."

"Hi," I said.

"How are you doing, Ford?"

"Doing well, Mr. Tucker. And yourself?"

"Myself is doing fine. And I've asked you to call me Dave. That Mr. Tucker business makes me feel like an old man."

Ford chuckled. "Sorry. What brings you to the sale?"

Grandpa told him about the dining room furniture he was there to see. "What about you?"

"Estate sales are often excellent sources of rare and vintage books."

When we got inside, I glimpsed a sewing room. I turned to Grandpa.

"Go," he said, with a grin. "I'll catch up with you in a few minutes."

I wove through the crowd to the room where the *piece de resistance* was a 1939 Singer 201 sewing machine. I was tempted to buy it, just to display it in Designs on You, but I couldn't justify the extravagance when I was just starting out and owed Grandpa for my start-up costs.

I moved on to a tin filled with beautiful buttons, many of which I was sure were antiques. This, I could afford, and I snapped it up before another buyer could beat me to it.

I stepped back into the living room to look for Grandpa. I didn't see him, but I did find myself standing beside George Meacham.

"Mr. Meacham! What a nice surprise!"

He smiled broadly. "Hello, pretty dressmaker!"

"Is Mrs. Meacham here?" I asked.

Looking like a mischievous child, he shook his head. "I'm here with Roscoe. We're looking for something nice to get for Mother."

"How sweet of you."

Gayle Leeson

Grandpa joined us then, and I introduced them.

"Your daughter is very pretty and very kind," George said. "She made a dress for my mother."

"Amanda does make some beautiful clothes. I imagine your mother looks lovely in the dress," Grandpa said.

"She does. She truly does." George's face abruptly clouded. "I miss Mother. I want to go home and see her."

I was glad that Brett showed up then because I didn't know how to respond to Mr. Meacham's last statement. I didn't want to say anything that would upset him.

"Hey, buddy! I wondered where you'd wandered off to," Brett said, with a nod at me. "Amanda...Mr. Tucker, hi. Good to see you again."

"Nice to see you too," I said.

Grandpa and Brett exchanged pleasantries, and then Grandpa said he needed to go get the truck to load the dining room set he'd bought. "I also bought a chifforobe that I'm confident I can restore into a beautiful piece."

"We need to run too," Brett said to George. "We'll be in big trouble with Melba if we're late."

George tsked. "Melba worries too much."

We waved goodbye to George and Brett and then hurried to Grandpa's truck. I was relieved that the sellers had plenty of help to load the furniture. I just wondered what we'd do when we got it home.

When we got to Grandpa's house, I realized that this wasn't Grandpa's first estate sale. The man was a pro. He had a truck ramp, a dolly, and furniture sliders on hand to get the furniture out of the truck and into his workshop.

Late that afternoon when we returned to my house, I invited Grandpa to play rummy. I put some pretzels in a bowl and moved the lilies from the center of the table to the island. I'd placed a sheet of aluminum foil underneath the vase so Jazzy wouldn't knock it over, and I made sure to move that to the island too.

Grandpa lifted a brow when he saw the flowers, but he didn't say anything...yet. I knew him too well to believe for an instant that he wasn't going to comment on them sooner or later.

I poured us some lemonade and then handed Grandpa the deck of cards.

As he shuffled and dealt the cards, I told him about Max not having enough energy to be present at Shops on Main all the time.

"I felt like a louse yesterday after I demanded to know where she'd been when I called to her after I first arrived. She said she thought she was a friend, not a servant and that she didn't know she was required to come when I summoned her."

"Did you apologize?"

"Of course." I sorted the seven cards in my hand. I had a pair of queens, an ace, a three and four in the same suit, and a two. I drew a five in the suit I needed and discarded the two.

"Then I'm confident that Max understood you were merely anxious over everything that had happened." Grandpa drew a card and then discarded a four. "Are you sure you want to remain at Shops on Main? I know you enjoy Max's company, but you can't risk your physical well-being or peace of mind being somewhere you don't feel safe."

"I know…but I want to give the situation more time. Now that the police are on to Janice, it's only a matter of time before they learn who her partners are and whether or not they had anything to do with Mark's death. Right?" I drew a six and discarded it.

"I hope so, Pup."

"Max said she left right after we did on Friday night, so she didn't see who gave the police entrance into the building and Janice's boutique."

Grandpa studied his cards before discarding a ten. "Unless the police have a key to the business, it was most likely Mrs. Meacham."

I frowned at him. "Why would the police have a key to Shops on Main?"

"That's how they did things in the olden days...back when I rode a dinosaur to school. The police had a key to every building in town."

"Oh, they did not."

He laughed. "I'm trying to throw you off your game. I have a feeling you're going to beat me this hand. But seriously, unless Mrs. Meacham has another person on whom she can rely in an emergency—Frank or one of the other vendors maybe—then she'd have to be the one to grant the police entry."

"Janice wasn't there yesterday." I drew another queen. "Do you suppose the police arrested her?"

"I don't know. Without finding the jewelry, I imagine they could question her but do little else. The search warrant for her shop wouldn't extend to her home. And, anyway, she'd be sure to hide it somewhere else before any other warrants could be obtained for her house and her car."

"So, you think she'll be back tomorrow?"

"I couldn't say." He nodded his head toward the flowers on the island. "Now why don't you tell me about your date?"

"It went well." I couldn't discard and displayed my cards to show Grandpa that I'd won.

He shook his head. "And me sitting here holding two aces. I'm glad I didn't have any money on this game."

We never gambled, but every time Grandpa lost, he said he was glad he didn't have any money on the game. And every time he won, he'd tell me I owed him a Coke.

I reveled in the game, the company, the peaceful camaraderie. I refused to think about tomorrow when who knew what would happen next at Shops on Main.

Chapter Twenty-One

On Monday morning, I was working on the final bridesmaid muslin when Janice came in. Max had been sitting at the desk in the reception area reading *A Tale of Two Cities* when Janice walked through the reception room door. The ghostly fashionista had just enough time to get to me and shout "Incoming" before the jewelry shop owner strode into the workshop.

"Good morning." Her tone was icy, and her eyes darted around the atelier rather than focusing on me.

I remained seated at the sewing machine. "Hi, Janice." I started to ask how she was doing or to make some other small talk, but it was apparent that she was here for a reason. I held my tongue, so she'd go ahead and get to the point of her visit.

"Mrs. Meacham said you and your grandfather were quick to help out on Friday night when my smoke detector went haywire."

I shrugged slightly. "I hope you'd do the same for me if you thought my shop was in jeopardy."

Max scoffed. "I highly doubt she would."

"The smoke alarm turned out to be the least of my worries on Friday." Janice finally pierced me with a hard stare. "Do you know what else happened?"

"What?"

"The police received an anonymous tip that there was stolen jewelry in my boutique."

"You're kidding!" I tried to force just enough incredulity into my tone and prayed my expression wouldn't betray me.

"Nope." She picked up the shears from the corner of the sewing machine table and ran her index finger along the edge.

Max gasped. "Don't you dare threaten us, you pillowcase!"

"Of course, when Brett let the police into the shop, they didn't find anything out of the ordinary."

"That's a relief," I said.

"A relief?" She slowly blinked.

"Well...sure. Everything was all right."

Janice leaned down closer to my face. "It wasn't all right. The police thought I was in possession of stolen property!"

My phone rang. I ignored it and said, "I'm sorry, but why are you ranting to me about it?"

"Because I want to know if you gave the police a false report against me."

"I most certainly did not." I backed my chair enough away from Janice that I could stand. "If you don't mind, I'd like you to leave so I can return to my work."

My phone continued to ring. I picked it up off the worktable and answered it, not daring to turn my back to Janice, who was still holding my shears and looking a bit deranged.

"Hello," I said, thinking it odd that there wasn't a number on my screen identifying the caller.

"Don't let that pillowcase make off with your scissors."

"Max?" My eyes darted around the room, but I didn't see her.

"Yes. I'm providing a distraction. Now, get those scissors and tell her to ankle on out of here."

I looked at Janice. "I need to take this call. I'd appreciate it if you'd put my shears back where you got them and ankle back upstairs."

Janice slammed the shears back onto the table and stormed out through the workshop door.

"It's bad luck not to leave through the same door you entered," Max said. "But that's fine. Maybe she needs some bad luck."

"And we need some good luck." I sank back onto my chair and rolled to the sewing machine. "She believes I ratted her out."

"But you didn't. Dave did."

"That doesn't matter. And, frankly, I'd rather she think it was me."

In an instant, Max's voice was coming from beside me rather than through the phone. "It'll be all right. I'm not about to let anything happen to you or to Dave."

"I appreciate the sentiment, but how are you going to prevent it?"

Before Max could answer, the atelier door opened. Thinking Janice was back, I whirled around. I breathed a sigh of relief when Connie walked in. She was carrying a mug and held it aloft as she strolled over to the sewing machine.

"I hope I'm not disturbing you, but I'm having some chamomile and thought I'd pop in to see if you'd like some."

"Thank you," I said with a smile, "but I've had my coffee so I should be in good shape for a while."

Connie gazed at the muslins hanging on the clothes rack behind me. "I'm looking forward to seeing the actual gowns. What color are they going to be?"

"Egyptian blue."

She drew her brows together. "Is that dark or light blue?"

"Somewhere between royal and navy. It's a gorgeous color."

"I can imagine." She took a sip of her tea before asking if I had a good weekend.

"I did. Grandpa and I went to an estate sale, and I bought a tin filled with buttons."

"I absolutely adore buttons," Connie said. "Do you have them here?"

"I do. If you can come back sometime this afternoon, we'll pour them all out and go through them."

"I'll be looking forward to it." She grinned. "By the way, please tell Dave I'm still trying to persuade my husband to let me have those new kitchen cabinets and that I believe I'm wearing him down."

I laughed. "I'll tell him."

An elegant woman who appeared to be in her late-fifties to early-sixties and had her light brown hair in an updo came into the reception area at about four o'clock that afternoon. She wore a black pantsuit and low-heeled pumps.

I'd heard the door open and came out of the atelier to greet her. "Hello, and welcome to Designs on You."

"Thank you." She smiled. "I saw that there was a new shop here and was curious. What do you do exactly?"

"I create custom clothing, mostly from vintage patterns. I really love styles from the 30s, 40s, and 50s especially."

"I see." She gave the reception area a dismissive glance. "Is this all you have?"

"At the moment. Most of the work I do is done on commission. For example, I'm currently making dresses for a wedding party."

She gave a not-so-elegant grunt and wandered over to look at the emerald gown that was on the mannequin.

"If you need help with anything, please let me know," I said.

As Ms. Updo browsed, a young mom—I guessed her to be in her early thirties—came in with a boy in tow. The boy appeared to be nine or ten years old and was wearing a denim backpack. At first glance, the backpack seemed to be trying to come alive, but I dismissed it as my eyes playing tricks on me. It was good I was taking a break from the sewing machine for a few minutes.

"Hi," said the mom to me, with a weary smile. She released the boy's hand and asked if he'd have a seat on one of the navy chairs by the window. "Mommy won't be long."

"I don't want to," the boy grumbled.

"Joey, please."

Her voice was firm now, and I imagined Joey understood that it meant business because he sat on one of the chairs.

"Grumpy little Gus, isn't he?" Max asked. "Although I'll take him over Ms. Snooty Britches any day."

I fought back a giggle and focused on the mom. "How can I help you?"

"My husband's company has a picnic every Labor Day, and most of the other wives look really cute and put-together. I always feel as if I look dowdy in comparison."

From the corner of my eye, I spotted a small, brown, furry head poking out of the top of Joey's backpack. My eyes widened and my jaw dropped.

What is that?

And then the animal was completely out of the backpack and running down Joey's arm. It was a ferret.

Joey laughed as an albino ferret joined its friend in escaping the backpack.

First, they were on Joey. Then they were on the floor. They were hopping forward, backward, and sideways.

"Weasels!" Max screeched.

"Joey Conrad, gather up Biscuits and Gravy right this instant!" Joey's mom demanded.

Apparently, like Jazzy, the ferrets could see Max. In an effort to get to her, one of them climbed Ms. Updo's back and snatched her hair off her head. Turns out, the updo was a wig. Ms. Updo screamed.

Gayle Leeson

"They're coming after me! Why are they after me?" Max yelled.

Awakened by the commotion, Jazzy prowled into the reception area from the atelier and crouched with her butt twitching in the air. Meanwhile, one of the ferrets—I briefly wondered if Biscuits or Gravy was the albino— made off with its prize while the other ferret tried to steal the wig from its pal. I didn't think the wig suited the coloring of either one, and I had no idea how to take control of this entire situation.

I watched helplessly as Ms. Updo tried to reclaim her hair, Joey and his mother tried to catch the ferrets, Max swatted at the "weasels," and Jazzy tried to decide whether she wanted to try and catch one of the ferrets or nab the wig. She must've decided the wig was the prize since the ferrets were engaging in a tug-or-war over it. She pounced and landed right in the middle of it.

Both ferrets hopped backwards and sideways as they weighed their odds against wrestling the wig away from the cat. But Ms. Updo was an opponent none of the three furballs had considered, and she reached down and grabbed the wig.

"I'll not be back in this circus of a shop again," Ms. Updo said with a huff as she stomped out, leaving the door open in her wake.

"No!" I cried.

Too little, too late. Both ferrets and Jazzy had taken off into the hall. Joey, his mom, and I ran after them.

The albino ferret skittered into Connie's shop as Jazzy chased the other one down toward Everthing Paper.

"Oh, hello!" Connie cooed, sweeping the animal into her arms. "Aren't you precious?"

Behind me, I heard Joey's mother thanking Connie for coming to the rescue. I followed Jazzy and Biscuit—or was it Gravy?—into Everything Paper.

"Frank, it's a wharf rat!" Ella's hand flew to her heart.

"No, it's just a ferret," I said.

The long, skinny creature shimmied up the counter and knocked over a jar of pencils. The noise caught its attention, and it grabbed a pencil between its teeth and ran over the register. Ella and Frank had an old-fashioned cash register to enhance the bygone atmosphere of their shop. The ferret hit just the right key or keys to make the drawer come sliding open. Pleased with this new development, the ferret took its front paws and flung coins out onto the floor as quickly as it could.

Jazzy hopped onto the counter.

"Frank, do something!"

"Like what, Ella?"

I reached for Jazzy. "One down."

Max was peering around from behind Frank.

"Hopefully, two down." It was Joey's mother. She reached for the ferret, missed, and it jumped to the floor and ran toward the back of the store.

"Darn it, Gravy! Get back here!"

So, that one was Gravy. There was one burning question answered. And, yet, there were so many more.

Joey's mom finally cornered Gravy, scooped it up, and returned it to Joey's backpack. She puffed out her cheeks and turned to Ella and Frank. "Did he destroy anything?"

Frank shook his head. "Livened up the morning, if you want the truth. He can even keep the pencil."

"Thanks."

Ella simply shook her head and began picking the coins up off the floor.

I walked with Joey's mom back into the hallway.

"I'm sorry about your other customer," she said.

"I don't think she was ever going to be my customer. And I have to agree with Frank—Biscuit and Gravy certainly did liven up the place."

She smiled. "I'll be back one day when Joey is at school."

I returned to Designs on You and closed the door behind me. I sat Jazzy onto floor and sank onto one of the navy chairs by the window.

Max appeared on the other one. "Frank and Ella are still having it out because she thought he should've captured the ferret. He's telling her he didn't want to get bit." She tried to mimic Frank's gravelly voice. "What if the thing had rabies, Ella? You ever think of that?"

I laughed. "That was wild."

"It was. I'm glad they gave Ms. Snooty Britches what for."

"I was calling her Ms. Updo in my mind."

"Not after the weasels got through with her." She threw back her head and chortled along with me.

Connie opened the door and eased inside. "I thought I heard you laughing."

I wiped tears from the corners of my eyes. "Is that terrible?"

"No." She smiled. "Ferrets are notorious thieves. They didn't make off with any of your buttons, did they?"

I shook my head. "The only treasures they discovered here was the wig of someone who I highly doubt was going to be a customer anyway and a pencil at Everything Paper."

"I saw the lady leave with her wig clenched in her fist. It was a nice wig. I didn't realize it was a wig while she was here."

"Neither did I." I rose and went over to the mantle where I'd placed the tin containing the buttons. I took the tin back, opened the lid, and poured some of the buttons onto the table between the two chairs.

Connie picked up one. "Oh, wow, Amanda. This one is enamel. Look how delicate it is."

It was delicate. It was a small white button with a pink rose surrounded by smaller blue flowers.

"It looks Victorian," I said, picking through the buttons to see if I could find another. I did and held it up for Connie to see.

In all, we found four of those. Since the buttons were small, I thought they would look best on a silk blouse or shirt dress.

We found some large, oval mother-of-pearl buttons as well as some silver buttons with dogwood blooms carved in the centers that I thought would look great on my denim jumpsuit.

As we pawed through the buttons discovering all the treasures the tin yielded, Connie said, "Oh, I almost forgot to tell you. Someone was in my shop earlier and said she heard on the radio that the police are asking for the public's help locating a stolen necklace. It disappeared from an estate sale yesterday."

My hands stilled. "Are you serious?"

"Yeah. You didn't steal a necklace while you were at the sale yesterday, did you?"

I shook my head. "Not me."

But who? A chill snaked down my spine as I wondered if someone else from Shops on Main had. And if that necklace was now upstairs at Janice's Jewelry.

Chapter Twenty-Two

Connie noticed my hands were trembling as she helped me get the buttons back into the tin. "Are you all right?"

"D-did Janice tell you what happened…here…on Friday night?"

"No."

"Janice's smoke alarm went off. Grandpa was here, and we went up to help Mrs. Meacham investigate."

"Was everything okay? I mean, I'm guessing it was…" Connie trailed off.

"It was a false alarm. Mrs. Meacham determined that the smoke detector needed a new battery. But, then, this morning, Janice came down here and accused me of falsely reporting to the police that she had stolen jewelry in her shop."

"What? That's ridiculous. Why would Janice even think that?"

"She thinks it because the police did come to Shops on Main on Friday night, and they searched her boutique," I said.

Connie gaped at me. "That's the first I've heard of it. But why does she think you had anything to do with the police investigating her?"

"I'm guessing she'd already spoken with Mrs. Meacham about it, and Mrs. Meacham said it wasn't her." I didn't trust Connie enough to give her the entire story. "And I did see that jewelry Janice said she'd made for one of her clients. You remember—she had such a conniption about it."

"She did, didn't she? And you think that jewelry is stolen?"

"I didn't say that." I chose my words carefully. "But it could be why Janice believes I'm the one who filed the false report."

"That could be." She snorted. "You didn't see her at the estate sale stuffing a necklace into her pocket, did you?"

"No...but Ford was there, and so were George and Brett Meacham."

Connie shook her head. "You don't think Ford or Brett would steal anything, do you? Ford is a good guy, and so is Brett. Brett handles everything after hours here at Shops on Main for Melba because she can't leave George at night." She patted my shoulder. "You'll get to know everybody in time. I think you're letting your imagination get the best of you because of...you know...Mark. And Janice might be doing the same thing."

I nodded. "You're probably right."

"It's quitting time, and I need to be getting home. Have a good night."

"You too."

Connie left but instead of hearing her footsteps recede to Delightful Home, I heard them going up the stairs. I looked up at the ceiling before closing my eyes to see if I could determine what direction she'd taken at the top of the staircase. Had she gone to see Janice, Mrs. Meacham, or Ford?

"I'll see what's going on," Max said softly.

I'd forgotten she was there. "Thank you."

I sat at the reception desk, took my calendar from the drawer, and called Heather. She answered right away.

"Hi, Heather. I've finished all the bridesmaids' muslins, and I wanted to see if you want to be here for their fittings. If so, I'll schedule the women to come in all at once."

"No," Heather said. "I don't need to see the muslins, but I do want to be there for the fitting when you have the finished gowns."

"All right. I'll have each of the women come in at their earliest convenience so that when the fabric gets here, I can make the dresses."

"Sounds terrific. I'm so glad you're doing this. And my grandma is thrilled about her dress too."

I just hoped I lived long enough to make Heather's bridesmaids' gowns and Ruby's dress. Janice—and now Connie—weren't making me feel very confident about that at the moment. Of course, I merely thanked Heather and ended the call.

Then I waited for Max to return with a report. She didn't. I couldn't just sit there, so I called one of the bridesmaids.

I scheduled Heather's sister to come in tomorrow around lunchtime, and then I waited again for Max. Nothing.

I was dialing another number when Max appeared.

I put down the phone. "Which one?"

"Ford. She told him everything you told her."

I gasped. "That rotten…" An appropriate word escaped me. "Person!"

"Dirty, back-stabbing bird is what she is," Max said. "That dame could take a mouthful of sugar and spit vinegar back in your face, that's what she could do."

"What does that even mean?" I asked.

"I don't know." She paced and waved her arms. "I'm so mad I could scream. But that wouldn't help matters. I've got to figure out what to do."

"You mean, we have to figure out what to do. What did Ford say to Connie?"

"He said he was afraid this was going to be a problem and that he'll take care of it."

"But—" I stopped, hearing footsteps on the stairs.

Max hurried over and stuck her head through the wall.

Ford flung open the door, and it would have hit Max if she'd had any substance.

"We need to talk," he said, closing the door behind him. He looked over into the atelier as if making sure there was no one there.

Max flew at him trying to hit him or scratch his face.

He rubbed his arms. "You keep it cold in here."

I merely stared at him. Max screamed in frustration.

"Okay." Ford put his hands on his hips to indicate he was ready to get down to business.

Before he could say anything further, the workshop door flew open, and Jason walked through the room and into the reception area. The man wore a smile as big as Texas, and I'd never felt so happy to see anyone in all my life.

"Hey, folks," Jason said.

"Save her!" Max yelled. "Punch him! Give him the ol' one-two!" She had her fists up now and was bobbing and weaving like a boxer.

"Is this where I come to get ferrets fetched, weasels wrangled, cats captured, dogs detained, rodents roped, and any other critters corralled?" Jason winked.

I laughed. As a matter of fact, I could hardly stop laughing.

Jason didn't appear to notice the edge of hysteria in my laughter because he elbowed Ford and winked at me. "Guess who I've been talking to?"

I wiped the corners of my eyes. "My money is on Frank."

"You got it. He told the story in great—and, I'm guessing, exaggerated—detail." He turned to Ford. "I assume you're here giving Amanda a hard time over it too."

"Over what?" Ford asked.

"The ferrets." Jason shook his head. "Go talk with Frank. But maybe get him away from Ella first. I get the feeling she doesn't appreciate the story the way he does." He chuckled. "Amanda, I've come to ask you to go to dinner with me and tell me the truth about the famed ferret fiasco."

"I'd love to." I looked at Ford. "Ford, go ahead and finish what you were saying."

"Oh, yeah, man, I'm sorry I interrupted," Jason said.

I'm not.

Max echoed the sentiment.

"It can wait," Ford said. "You two have fun. I think I need to see if Frank and Ella have left yet."

After Ford left, Jason said he'd go upstairs and lock the door and be right back.

"I need to take Jazzy home. Would it be all right if we meet at the restaurant?"

"Sure." He smiled, suggested a place, and when I agreed, said he'd see me there.

"I don't want you to meet him there," Max said. "I want him to be with you every step of the way. And then seduce him so he'll spend the night with you."

"Max!"

"What? I want you to be safe."

"I'll be fine."

"You could stay with Dave," she said.

"I'll be fine," I repeated.

She sighed. "Be careful."

"I will be."

After regaling Jason with the ferret story—which he swore was even better than Frank's version because Frank didn't even know about the wig—he and I finished our dinner and said goodnight. As I drove home, I thought about everything I'd learned about the people at Shops on Main since opening Designs on You. I tried to stick to facts and not speculate…at least, not too much.

Mark Tinsley was having trouble making ends meet and was going to have to give up his space at Shops on

Main. His father was in a costly assisted living facility. Mark kept his relationship with his father a secret from his mother. Mark was shot to death in his office.

Janice and Mark had been dating. Mark had told his mother about Janice. Janice had at some point also been dating Guy. I had no idea whether Janice had dated the other man before, after, or during the time she dated Mark. Guy wasn't all that young—in fact, I'd imagine he was fairly close to Janice in age—but Connie said Janice enjoyed dating younger men to boost her self-esteem. Of course, if she was dating a young man who couldn't afford to buy her nice things, then she might have been two-timing with an older man who had money. But that was conjecture. Moving on.

When I'd discovered the "good" jewelry Max had told me was in the drawer, Janice had blown her top. Then she'd lied about the jewelry having been custom made for one of her clients. That was implausible when she told it, but now that we'd seen the manufacturers' marks on some of the jewelry, we knew for certain it was a lie. That meant Janice had either stolen the jewelry herself or was holding it for the thief.

Grandpa had reported the stolen jewelry, and it had disappeared before the police could search Janice's Jewelry. Brett had unlocked the door to Shops on Main and to Janice's Jewelry that night to let the police in.

A memory of George Meacham giving me an impish grin and saying, "Roscoe has sticky fingers" flooded my mind. Had George been talking about his brother in the past tense or his brother—Brett—in the present tense?

Brett had unlocked the door. He could've gotten there sooner and removed the jewelry from Janice's shop. He could have easily gone back outside and waited for the officers to arrive. Plus, he was a younger man. And, again, Janice enjoyed dating younger men.

But what about Ford? And Connie? How were they involved in all this? If everyone was involved and the police arrested them, how would it affect Shops on Main? That is, unless one of them killed me like they did Mark, and then carried on with their business as usual.

When I got home, I sprinted into the house and immediately locked the door behind me. Then I made sure the back door and all the windows were locked too.

Jazzy was lying on the sofa. I gathered her into my lap and was reassured slightly when she started purring. I called Grandpa Dave, but he didn't answer. I thought he was probably out in the workshop working on the furniture he'd bought yesterday.

But Janice knew Grandpa was in her shop on Friday night. She might blame him for the police searching her shop. I called again. Still no answer. I kissed the top of Jazzy's head, placed her back onto the cushion beside me, grabbed my keys, and headed out the door.

Chapter Twenty-Three

I drove as quickly as I dared to Grandpa's house, threw my car into park, and got out. I left the door standing open as I raced onto the porch. I tried the front door. It was unlocked, so I hurried inside.

"Grandpa!" I frantically looked into the living room and kitchen before looking out the kitchen window to see that there was a light on in the workshop. I went out the back door and sprinted to the workshop.

There was Grandpa Dave, wearing noise-canceling headphones while he used a belt sander on the chifforobe he'd bought yesterday. He was whistling *Tennessee Waltz*.

He caught a glimpse of me as I heaved a sigh of relief. He turned off the sander and removed the headphones. "Hey, Pup. Everything all right? You look white as a sheet."

"Let me run back out and turn my car off," I said.

When I returned from properly parking my car and shutting the engine off, Grandpa was concerned. I told him I'd tried to call and that when he didn't answer, I was afraid something had happened to him.

His shoulders slumped. "I'm so sorry. I didn't mean to worry you."

"That doesn't matter now. All that matters is that you're all right."

He gave me a one-armed hug and nodded toward the chifforobe. "I sanded the finish off the tables and chairs this morning. I'm going to use the same varnish on all of them so that maybe I can sell them together."

"Good thinking," I said. "Hey, I'll let you get back to it. I just wanted to make sure you were okay."

"Nonsense. Come in and let's have something cold to drink."

I considered this, but I knew that if I stayed, I'd end up telling Grandpa everything that had happened today with Janice, Connie, and Ford. That would only worry him. "I need to get back. I have to schedule bridesmaid fittings."

"All right then. Maybe I can come by and bring you lunch tomorrow."

"Sounds good to me. You be careful in here."

"I will, Pup. And I'll keep a closer eye on my phone."

My car and my heartbeat were considerably slower on the drive back home. I'd been so afraid that Janice or one of her partners had gotten to Grandpa and had accused him of turning them into the police. Of course, he would admit to it and say that I had no knowledge of it whatsoever. He'd want to protect me at all costs. I understood that feeling of wanting to protect a loved one well.

When I walked up to my front door, I got out my key to unlock it. It wasn't locked. In fact it was slightly ajar. I groaned. Had I been in such a hurry to get to Grandpa Dave that I'd neglected to shut the door all the way? No...I was certain I'd locked it. Hadn't I?

I felt a prickle at the back of my neck as I pushed open the door. My blood turned cold when I saw Brett Meacham sitting on my sofa. Jazzy was nowhere in sight. I imagined she'd ran and hid when he'd broken into the house.

"What are you doing here?" I asked. "How did you know where I live?" My mind was racing with a dozen additional questions, but those are the ones that came out of my mouth first.

"You seem to forget my grandmother is your landlord. I know all about you, Amanda. What I need to know is what you know about me."

"I don't know anything about you." I spotted a pistol in his right hand. He had it casually on his lap, but it was pointing at me.

"I believe you do. Start talking."

"All right. I think you and Janice are working together to sell jewelry."

"Stolen jewelry?" he asked.

I shrugged. "You tell me."

Gayle Leeson

He barked out a laugh. "That's not how this works. I'm the one with the gun. You're the one doing the talking. Who have you told that you think I'm selling stolen jewelry?"

"No one."

"I know better. You've told your grandpa at the very least. Janice said he was with you in her shop on Friday night."

"We were in there," I said. "We followed your grandmother in there when the alarm went off. That's all."

"I don't believe you."

I saw that he wasn't going to buy the story that I hadn't told anyone anything, so I went with what I felt was my best option. "Fine. The only person who knows about the stolen jewelry is my friend Max."

"Max who?"

"Max Englebright. She comes into Shops on Main often."

Brett narrowed his eyes. "I've never met her."

"She's...elusive. But she's a jewelry aficionado. I didn't even suspect that the jewelry was stolen until I described the bracelet I'd found in Janice's shop to Max," I said, warming to my subject. "Max knew right away that the piece was made by Tiffany & Co. in the 1920s."

"So? How did she know it was stolen?"

"I don't know. You'd have to ask her that."

He stood and waved the gun. "Fine. Let's go ask her."

I had no idea where I'd take Brett to make him think we were going to see Max Englebright, but at least, I'd bought myself some time.

Brett walked over to me, turned me around, and pushed me onto the front porch just as a police car pulled into my driveway and blocked my car. I saw that Grandpa's truck was parked on the side of the road across from my house. I couldn't see whether or not he was in the vehicle, but I prayed he'd stay inside it, keep his head down, and not get hurt.

Officer Cranston got out of the car. He drew his service weapon but stayed behind the car door to give himself some cover. "Mr. Meacham, things will go much better for you if you allow Ms. Tucker to walk over here to me."

"No way." Brett put his arm around my waist and placed the gun barrel against my head. "I let her go, and you'll shoot me."

"I give you my word that I won't do that."

"Like your word means that much to me at this point."

There was a rustle in the bushes to my right. I whipped my head around. Brett apparently did the same thing and relaxed his hold on the gun. Then, before I knew what was happening, Brett was crumpling onto the porch like a sack of potatoes. I kicked the gun out of his reach.

"Hope I didn't hit him too hard," Grandpa Dave said, looking at the crowbar he held.

Officer Cranston hurried over and cuffed Brett, whose eyes were rolling back in his head.

"Is he going to be all right?" I asked.

"Yeah," Officer Cranston said. "He'll just have a whopper of a headache. Good job, Dave."

I looked over toward the bushes. "What--?"

"Oh, yeah. I'll need to find your TV remote."

I smiled when I realized that's what he'd thrown into the bushes and deflated against his shoulder. "Thank goodness you were here."

"Thank goodness I got your text."

"What text?"

"The text you sent telling me Brett had your address and you were afraid you were in danger."

"I didn't send a text." I looked to make sure Officer Cranston was out of earshot. He'd hoisted the wobbly Brett Meacham to his feet and had taken him over to sit in the back of the squad car. "Do you think Max sent it from the tablet I gave her?"

"I guess anything's possible."

When I walked through the door to Shops on Main on Tuesday morning, Ford was there. I got the feeling he'd been watching for me because he enveloped me in a bear hug.

"Good morning to you too," I said.

"Here." He took Jazzy's carrier. "Let me get this for you." He walked with me to Designs on You.

I unlocked the door, walked inside, and reached for the carrier. Ford sat it on the floor, and I let Jazzy out. She gave him a wary look as she walked away from him.

"I'm glad you're all right," Ford said.

"I am too." I frowned slightly. "Is what happened to me last night common knowledge around here already?"

"I'm sure it will be soon. Reese Cranston, the officer who arrested Brett, is my brother-in-law. He's had me keeping an eye on Janice since Mark's murder."

"Because they were romantically involved?"

"No, because Mark had a file on his computer indicating he'd discovered a piece of expensive jewelry in her shop. When questioned about it, Janice told Mark she'd acquired it at an estate sale for a wealthy client. Mark pressed her on the matter, but he couldn't get her to disclose her client's name."

"Let me guess. No client?"

"No one who was above board at any rate. Mark did a deep web search for that particular piece of jewelry and learned that it had been reported stolen. Mark then went to

Janice and demanded twenty-five percent of the profits from the sale of the stolen jewelry to keep silent about what he'd found."

"Gee. He was more reasonable than most people would've been," I said.

"Really. But Mark had noted that twenty-five percent of the proceeds at the jewelry's projected sale price would have paid his father's assisted living expenses for three months." Ford blew out a breath. "He wrote that the day before he was shot."

"That's incredible. And sad to think that if Janice and Brett hadn't been so greedy and Mark so desperate to care for his father, Mark would still be alive."

"And they'd still be in business, but that's neither here nor there."

I lowered my eyes. "I thought you were involved."

"I know. But I couldn't risk Janice finding out I was working against her." He spread his hands. "I told Connie when Reese first came to me because I felt I had to tell somebody. And I'd known Connie longer than anyone else here."

"You were coming to tell me yesterday afternoon?" I asked.

He nodded. "After Connie told me Janice had threatened you, I'd come down to caution you. Reese said that although they were closing in on a suspect, they still didn't have enough evidence to make an arrest. But then I kept quiet because I thought that since you were going to be with Jason, you'd be all right."

"What about the hollowed-out books?" I asked.

"I used those to pass flash drives to Reese."

"That's clever."

He grinned. "We thought so. You were even wise to that. How did you know?"

I shrugged. "A little bird told me."

Ford laughed. "Well, I'm glad you're all right. I'd better get to work."

Max hadn't made an appearance all morning, and I was concerned about her. It wasn't unusual for her to be absent in the mornings, but I wondered how much energy it had taken her to send that text to Grandpa Dave.

Mrs. Meacham called me at about ten-thirty that morning and asked me to come to her office at my earliest convenience.

I took a deep breath before I started up the stairs. *This is it. She's going to make me leave because Grandpa Dave beaned Brett with a crowbar.*

I tapped lightly on the office door and entered when I heard Mrs. Meacham's curt "Come in."

"How's Brett?" I asked her.

She waved her hand toward one of the chairs facing her desk, indicating I should sit. "He's fine. He has a slight concussion. The hospital kept him overnight for observation. I've just come from there."

I sat and folded my hands in my lap. "I'm really sorry. Grandpa tried not to hit him too hard."

"Well, I appreciate that. I'm sorry your grandfather had to take that action and that Brett behaved so abominably." She removed her glasses and rubbed her eyes. "I'm disappointed in Brett and furious with that Jezebel who lured Brett into this criminal behavior."

I nodded. I'd already heard from Grandpa earlier that Officer Cranston had called and let him know that the gun Brett had at my house was suspected to be the same one that killed Mark Tinsley. Cranston felt certain that the ballistics report would confirm that suspicion. The police had also turned up the pouch of stolen jewelry at Brett's apartment along with an addition—the necklace taken from the estate sale on Sunday. But if Mrs. Meacham wanted to see Janice as the villain in the entire affair, I couldn't blame her. In her position, I'd rather think some pillowcase was responsible for a man's murder than my own grandson.

I told Mrs. Meacham that if there was anything I could do to help to please let me know. We'd later learn that Brett and Janice had both taken plea deals in exchange for reduced sentences. When I found that out, I was relieved I wouldn't have to testify against my landlord's grandson.

Jason's door was open when I left Mrs. Meacham's office, and I stopped by to say hello.

He hurried over to me. "Ford just told me what happened. I was on my way down to see you. Are you okay?"

I smiled. "I'm fine."

He kissed me then—our first real kiss—and he didn't stop until someone cleared her throat. It was his client, and although I could feel my cheeks turning redder than a tomato, Jason didn't seem to mind.

Max was sitting on the desk in the reception area when I returned to Designs on You. She was swinging her legs. Jazzy was watching her contentedly.

"Aren't you the berries?" She winked.

"You are the berries, and am I glad to see you!"

She threw back her head and laughed. "I didn't know what to do when I saw Brett in Mrs. Meacham's office copying down your address. But then I remembered that the tablet you gave me has a little photograph of an envelope on it. I opened the envelope, and it had a bunch of names in it. I didn't see yours, so I sent a message to

Dave. I prayed he'd get the message and that he'd know what to do."

"Thanks to you, he knew exactly what to do." I grinned. "Are you ever the elephant's eyebrows!"

Author's Notes

Thank you kindly!

First off, I want to thank **you** for taking the time to read this book. I also want to thank my wonderful beta readers Lianna Trent, Rachel Vance, Kris Sheets, Carrie Schmidt, Marcy Barth, Amy Connolley, Sally Schmidt, Barbara Hackel, Linda Bergstrom, and Meg Gustafson for taking their time to read and provide valuable feedback. A very special shout out to Karen "Lovey" Borelli, a comedic genius. If you enjoyed the frenetic ferrets, you have her to thank for providing the inspiration. Thanks to Andrea, Garry, and Will of Twin Roses Design for showing me around their studio and sharing their stories with me. Thanks to Garic Stephens of Lavelle for showing me around his atelier and answering my many questions. (It did my heart good to see a note from his mom reminding him to "Eat something" above his worktable. We moms don't care how grown up our children are, they're still our children.) Thank you to Marie Bridgeforth, for designing such a beautiful cover. Thanks to Robert Weisfeld for permitting me artistic license with regard to *The Abingdon Virginian's* archives. And, last but certainly not least, thank you to the residents of the Greenway-Trigg building (Olive Oil Company employees and R. Dean Barr) for welcoming me into your shops.

Shops on Main

The fictional Shops on Main is loosely based on the Greenway-Trigg building in Abingdon, Virginia. The building was constructed in 1864 and has been a private home, a retail establishment, and—as an Olive Oil Company employee told me—a "beehive." I didn't know what that meant but learned that it was a bordello. I used to love visiting the bookstore housed inside the building when I worked up the street from Greenway-Trigg. I'd take my lunch hour to walk to the store, browse, and then sit on the swing outside with my find.

Prohibition/Poison Alcohol?

I got my information for this part of *Designs on Murder* primarily from a *Slate* article dated February 19, 2010 titled *The Chemist's War*. The article tells the "little-told story of how the United States government poisoned alcohol during Prohibition with deadly consequences."

When people continued to consume a lot of alcohol despite it being banned, government officials ordered industrial alcohols manufactured in the United States to have the addition of lethal chemicals. This was because crime syndicates were stealing massive quantities of industrial alcohol used in paints, solvents, fuels, and medical supplies and redistilling it to drink. The U. S. Treasury Department estimated that by the mid-1920s, some 60 million gallons of industrial alcohol were stolen annually.

The most common additive was methyl alcohol, and by mid-1927, the new denaturing formulas included kerosene, brucine, gasoline, benzene, cadmium, iodine, zinc, mercury salts, nicotine, ether, formaldehyde, chloroform, camphor, carbolic acid, quinine, and acetone.

Rachel, one of my brilliant beta readers, pointed out that Johnson City, Tennessee (about an hour's drive from Abingdon) was called *Little Chicago* during the time of Prohibition because the city was reputed to be an occasional hideout for gangsters, including Al Capone. If you're interested, you can read more about it at https://bit.ly/2UV3GUq.

1920s Jewelry

While the 1920s is considered one of the most important eras in fashion history, it is also said to be one of the most important periods in the history of jewelry design during the Art Deco movement.

Cartier is one of the most famous Art Deco jewelry designers. Louis François Cartier founded the company in 1847. Two generations later, his grandsons Pierre, Louis, and Jacques turned the Parisian watchmaking company into a global jewelry design business. Incidentally, the Cartier building on Fifth Avenue in New York is reputed to have been bought for $100 and a string of pearls!

Tiffany & Co. was founded in 1837 and is one of the most famous Art Deco jewelry designers in the world. The first Tiffany & Co. store was opened on Broadway by Charles Lewis Tiffany and John B. Young to sell stationery and "fancy goods" (like lamp shades, I imagine). They later incorporated jewelry design, and the rest is history. If you're a football fan, you probably already know that Tiffany & Co. creates the Vince Lombardi Trophy.

J. E. Caldwell died in 1881 and the company officially closed in 2003. However, their rare vintage Art Deco jewelry has been known to bring as much as $120,000 on the open market.

Bailey, Banks, and Biddle—founded in 1832—is considered to be America's oldest jewelry company. By the late 1860s, this company was considered the finest jewelry maker in America. Bailey, Banks, and Biddle produced military medals and swords, and the firm designed the Great Seal of the United States.

Mario Buccellati opened his first store in Milan in 1819 and quickly rose to prominence among jewelry designers. After establishing shops in Milan, Rome, and Florence, the company set up shop on Fifth Avenue in New York and later in Palm Beach, Florida. Buccellati's artwork is on display at the Chianciano Art Museum in Tuscany.

ABOUT THE AUTHOR

Gayle Leeson is a pseudonym for Gayle Trent. I also write as Amanda Lee. As Gayle Trent, I write the Daphne Martin Cake Mystery series and the Myrtle Crumb Mystery series. As Amanda Lee, I write the Embroidery Mystery series. To eliminate confusion going forward, I'm writing under the name Gayle Leeson only. My family and I live in Virginia near Abingdon, Virginia, and I'm having a blast with this new series.